YEARLING BOOKS

Since 1966, Yearling has been the

leading name in classic and award-winning

literature for young readers.

With a wide variety of titles,

Yearling paperbacks entertain, inspire,

and encourage a love of reading.

VISIT

WWW.RANDOMHOUSE.COM/KIDS

**TO FIND THE PERFECT BOOK, PLAY GAMES,
AND MEET FAVORITE AUTHORS!**

OTHER YEARLING BOOKS YOU WILL ENJOY

PURE DEAD BATTY
Debi Gliori

COUNT KARLSTEIN
Philip Pullman

VICKY ANGEL
Jacqueline Wilson

THE FAIRY REBEL
Lynne Reid Banks

THE UNSEEN
Zilpha Keatley Snyder

SPACE RACE
Sylvia Waugh

HECK

WHERE THE BAD KIDS GO

DALE E. BASYE

ILLUSTRATIONS BY **BOB DOB**

A YEARLING BOOK

THIS BOOK IS DEDICATED TO MY SON, OGDEN,
WHO MADE MY BELIEF IN THE IMPOSSIBLE POSSIBLE

Text copyright © 2008 by Dale E. Basye
Illustrations copyright © 2008 by Bob Dob

All rights reserved. Published in the United States by Yearling, an imprint of Random House Children's Books, a division of Random House, Inc., New York. Originally published in hardcover by Random House Books for Young Readers, an imprint of Random House Children's Books, New York, in 2008.

Yearling and the jumping horse design are registered trademarks of Random House, Inc.

Visit us on the Web! www.randomhouse.com/kids

Educators and librarians, for a variety of teaching tools, visit us at www.randomhouse.com/teachers

The Library of Congress has cataloged the hardcover edition of this work as follows:
Basye, Dale E.
Heck : where the bad kids go / by Dale E. Basye ; illustrated by Bob Dob.
p. cm.
Summary: When timid Milton and his older, scofflaw sister Marlo die in a marshmallow bear explosion at Grizzly Mall, they are sent to Heck, an otherworldly reform school from which they are determined to escape.
ISBN 978-0-375-84075-3 (trade) — ISBN 978-0-375-94075-0 (lib. bdg.) — ISBN 978-0-375-84988-6 (e-book)
[1. Brothers and sisters—Fiction. 2. Behavior—Fiction. 3. Future life—Fiction.
4. Reformatories—Fiction. 5. Schools—Fiction. 6. Humorous stories.] I. Dob, Bob, ill. II. Title.
PZ7.B2938Hec 2008 [Fic]—dc22 2007008379

ISBN: 978-0-375-84076-0 (pbk.)

Printed in the United States of America

20 19 18 17 16 15 14 13 12

First Yearling Edition

 CONTENTS

FOREWORD

As many believe, there is a place above and a place below. But there are also places in between. Some not quite awfully perfect and others not quite perfectly awful.

Building infinite eternities is a costly endeavor, even for the Galactic Order Department. That's why the Powers That Be (and any of its associated or subsidiary enterprises, including—but not limited to—the Powers That Be Evil) have to be resourceful, stitching together spaces between spaces, places between places.

They are all around you and go by many names. Some feel like eternity. And some of them actually are eternity . . . at least for a little while . . .

1 · LAST WRONGS

IN GENERICA, KANSAS, Christmas wasn't something you felt in the chill of the winter air or the warmth of a generous smile. It was announced by the sixteen-foot tower of crystal angels at Grizzly Mall—the Mall of Generica.

And this year was no different—at first. Exhausted shoppers filed by, momentarily entranced by the shimmering, heart-faced, bare-bottomed cupids. That is, until Marlo Fauster smashed them to bits with the oar she'd stolen from Spoiled Sports Sporting Goods.

"Let's go!" shrieked Marlo, a blue-haired, thirteen-going-on-thirty-year-old girl, to her gangly younger brother, Milton. Shards of shining wings and harps rained down around them.

The two children bounded across the showroom floor, Marlo running with a look of fierce determination and Milton running out of pure fear. Unbeknownst to both of them, they were also running out of time.

Milton had spent most of his young life avoiding trouble: staring at his shoes, shuffling along unnoticed, ducking away from tense—or even remotely interesting— situations for fear of their potentially dangerous potential. He only felt truly safe when tucked between the covers of a book, experiencing life secondhand.

Marlo, however, was a different story.

Too far was where Marlo lived. If something didn't involve petty (and not-so-petty) crime, it just wasn't worth doing.

Maybe it was all just a cry for attention. Unfortunately, Marlo's latest acts of thievery and vandalism were drawing far *too* much attention. At least that's how Milton saw it through his thick, Coke-bottle glasses as his sister dragged him toward his untimely demise.

They ran past stunned shoppers into the mall concourse, Marlo waving her oar as if rowing furiously through a human sea. Milton fought to keep up.

"That should buy us some time from security!" Marlo squealed with manic glee. It was at times like this, Milton thought, that he was in the presence of— and grudgingly related to—a new kind of evil.

"And you should have *bought* that stupid oar!" Milton replied, panting.

"Why would I buy an oar?" she asked, giving Milton's arm a sadistic twist. "We live in Kansas, short bus."

The two siblings darted around a corner and burst into the Grizzly Mall food court.

"Then w-why . . . ?" Milton stammered in front of Tongue Thaied.

"For the sport of it," Marlo said with pride. "If I pull this off—the most conspicuous holiday heist in Grizzly Mall history—I'll be a modern-day Kleptopatra." She paused dramatically, her dark eyes twinkling with reflected Christmas lights. "The stuff of shoplifting legend. And all that expensive makeup is just icing on the cake."

Milton stared at the pink Goodbye Puppy bag underneath his arm as he trotted onward.

"So all this makeup . . . you didn't need me to just hold it for you back at the cosmetics counter . . . I . . . I just stole . . . *lip gloss*?"

"And Suburban Blight cheek bronzer with free-radical scavengers and lipid-rich amino moisturizers," Marlo said while descending an ascending escalator. She grinned. "Welcome to the life, my gullible little apprentice. You are but putty in my skillful hands."

Behind them, a full-bodied mall security guard lumbered in hot pursuit. Another chunky-style defender of mall law soon joined him, slurping down a smoothie.

Milton looked behind him. Despite their weight being nearly double their IQ, the guards were closing in.

"I can't believe you tricked me into stealing for

you!" Milton barked in his squeaky, just-turned-eleven voice.

Marlo snickered. The fact that she could run clad in several layers of black thrift-store dresses, holding an eight-foot oar, and *still* manage to maintain a superior attitude was impressive.

"You might get all the A's in the family, but I certainly aced *you*," she snorted, her black lips catching on a fang.

Milton and Marlo rushed into the mall's massive atrium, joining a crowd gathered around a white, globby sculpture. A fierce marshmallow bear, frozen in mid-attack, loomed over the horde of gawking Genericans. Below the twenty-foot-tall sugary bruin was a banner declaring "Welcome to Grizzly Mall: Home of the State's Second-Largest Bear-Themed Marshmallow Statue!"

Marlo's oar sliced through the mass of shoppers like a thin, wooden shark fin.

"Try to blend," she whispered to her trembling brother.

Milton squished the pink bag of lipstick, fruit-scented creams, and vials of pricey gosh-knows-whats under his armpit. Despite the heat radiating from the mob, Milton shivered. Something—or someone—was near, something so cold that it robbed the heat from his very bones. He squinted through his thick glasses and noticed a dark smudge. He wiped his lenses, but the stubborn smudge was still there, hovering on the edge of the crowd that filled the atrium. The dark smudge was a boy.

A hulking boy. A cruel boy. A boy all too familiar to Milton. A boy who, in many ways, resembled a smudge. A boy whose eyes were dull, dark, wicked slits. A boy whose skin was like puffy, freckled dough that gave off a sickly sweet smell like rotting fruit. A boy named Damian.

Damian sneered at Milton and ran his grubby finger across his throat as he lurched from the mall commons into the heart of the mall. Milton gulped and shut his eyes. On the insides of his eyelids, however, he replayed scenes of Damian's notorious cruelty, all of which—unfortunately—starred Milton.

Scene One: The boys' locker room just after gym class. Damian, clad in stained, crunchy underwear, flicks a towel at Milton. It slices through the air like a terry-cloth snake, hissing and snapping, stinging Milton's scrawny body.

Scene Two: The school hallway. Milton runs, wheezing. Damian rushes up behind him. He thrusts his hands deep into Milton's baggy corduroys and emerges with Milton's Stargate: Atlantis *underwear. He yanks them up to Milton's neck. The pain is enough to postpone puberty for a year.*

Scene Three: Mid-Kansas Junior Science Championship.

Milton stands proud by his science project: a generator pow-ered by two ferrets on twin wheels. Milton's braces gleam as he smiles for the teacher's camera. A flashbulb goes off. His project explodes. Bits of burning metal fly into the air. Chil-dren shriek. Singed ferrets shriek. Damian shrieks with laughter as he stuffs several fat firecrackers back into the pocket of his filthy jeans.

Milton opened his eyes. What upset Milton wasn't necessarily that Damian was here in Grizzly Mall. It was that he actually looked guilty. It was a look Milton had never seen on the front of Damian's great, lumpy head before. What this meant to Milton was that Damian was up to something that scared even *him,* something unequaled in his reign of thuggery. The thought made Milton's head hurt.

"Oww!" he yelped as Marlo whacked him in the back of his head with her stolen oar.

"Wake up, runt. We've got company."

A fresh quartet of security guards lurched out of the food court, sloshing Huge Gulps and munching curly fries, to aid their winded comrades. One of them jabbed a fry toward Milton and Marlo. The guards broke into pairs and approached the shoplifting duo from either side.

In the blink of her eye, Marlo seized Milton by the arm and dragged him into the center of the crowd.

"W-what the . . . ?" Milton stammered.

"I've got it under control," she replied.

"I'm doomed . . . ," Milton mumbled under his breath.

Marlo stopped just in front of the marshmallow bear and shoved the oar under her brother's neck.

"Don't come any closer!" she shouted, her nostrils flaring. "I mean it!"

The crowd froze. The plump security guards, however, continued their approach.

Marlo grabbed a small pot of sickly blue makeup from the stolen cosmetics bag and held it up to Milton's clammy, pale face. "So help me, I will apply this eye shadow that so clearly doesn't complement his complexion!"

Milton's pet ferret, Lucky, chose this moment to pop his fuzzy white head out of Milton's backpack, where he often hid, fell asleep, and awakened in strange new places. Lucky considered the crowd with his bright pink eyes and gave his opinion of the situation with a dry hiss.

The crowd backed away as one, like a giant creature with a hundred heads. Even the security guards stopped insecurely in their tracks. Everyone was taken aback by the sudden, inexplicable appearance of the twitchy white weasel-like animal—except for the Fausters, who were unaware that they were harboring a stowaway.

"Wow," Marlo whispered as she scanned the scene with awe. "I had no idea how style conscious our town was."

Milton heard a faint sizzling sound coming from behind the bear. Curious, he turned his head—as much as he could with an oar wedged beneath his neck—and saw Damian smirking from the balcony, just above the bear. Milton followed Damian's gaze down toward a thin plume of smoke snaking out of the bear's white glob of a tail.

Damian had lodged a stick of dynamite in a place no real grizzly would tolerate. The violated sculpture gave off the smell of a roasting s'more.

Milton's eyes bugged out. He broke free of his sister's clutches and ran.

"Hey!" Marlo tried to chase after her brother. Unfortunately, the hem of her dress stuck fast to the marshmallow grizzly's gummy paw. She pulled at clawlike strings of gooey taffy but couldn't get away. Milton looked back and saw his sister struggling.

"Leave the dress!" he shouted.

"Are you kidding?" Marlo sneered. "This is vintage. *One of a kind.*"

Milton ran back and tugged her sleeve. "C'mon! The bear's gonna blow!"

Marlo's face looked like a bowl of sour milk with makeup. "I'd sooner *die* than leave this—"

The sputtering fuse disappeared into the bear's bottom and the massive marshmallow monument exploded. Grown men screamed. Women wept. Marlo and Milton, hand in hand, were instantly engulfed in flaming goo.

Smoke, noise, and burning marshmallow fused together to create a sickeningly sweet moment, one that was both ridiculously tragic and tragically ridiculous. It was a moment that Generica would talk about for years to come. Yet for Marlo and Milton, it was the last moment that they would ever share. On earth, anyway.

2 · WELCOME TO HECK, POPULATION: YOU

MILTON FELT LIKE someone had ripped a full-body Band-Aid off him, one that covered both sides of his skin, outside and in. Sure, you'd expect a fiery end at least to sting, but this sensation didn't exactly feel "physical." It made Milton feel like a weird echo of himself.

Milton had—at first—felt as if he was floating upward through clouds of fragrant mist, accompanied by a choir of angelic voices and the gorgeous swipes of a harp, with his sister uncharacteristically mute and still by his side. The sights and sounds were heavenly—like paradise—until Milton sensed a hesitation, a peculiar scrutiny. It was kind of like when he went to the dentist and they had to take X-rays. The assistant with her big lead apron aimed the gun-thing at your "full of bitter cardboard" cheek, then went away to flick on a secret switch. You didn't exactly feel the X-rays, but you kind of did. You knew that you were being analyzed in a deep way, like a thousand microscopic eyes were sifting through your every cell.

After that initial invasive tingle, there was the briefest of pauses. But then his ascension screeched to a jolting halt, like someone (or something) had changed his/her/its mind. Snippets of a conversation streamed into his head, as if he were a radio tuning into a faraway frequency.

"No . . . wait . . . *him* . . . perfect for the job . . ." After this snap judgment snapped, Milton pitched abruptly downward, due south, at a jillion miles an hour.

Marlo and Milton shrieked as they tumbled down a coiled slide enveloped in clouds of vapor. They glided for miles—thousands of miles, actually—screeching, their terrified faces still spotted with blobs of smoldering marshmallow.

With each twist of the slide, the white clouds of mist gradually darkened, at first to an ash gray, then finally a sooty black. The divine chorus of angelic harmonies grew fainter. In its place was the sound of mocking laughter.

After what seemed like hours but was actually no time whatsoever, since time holds no dominion over this particular place (though the Time Institute of Chronometry, Tabulation, and Order Know-how—

TIC-TOK—is making significant advances by the minute), they landed, whimpering, in a semi-deflated, Olympic-sized kiddie pool full of red Ping-Pong balls and rotting garbage.

Marlo rose unsteadily and wiped fresh trails of mascara tears off her pale cheeks. Milton moaned and straightened his glasses. One of the lenses was broken. He squinted out of the good lens, looking like a runtish, well-read Cyclops.

They cautiously stepped out of the garbage pool into a small, sweltering cavern filled with thick, greasy smoke—a cross between a giant's fireplace and the worst Upchucky Cheez restaurant *ever*. Above them, housing the spiral slide, was a towering stone chimney with no visible beginning. It was as if they had tumbled down a gargantuan garbage chute. Marlo wiped coffee grounds and moldy cottage-cheese clots off her dress in disgust.

To their left was a plastic cartoonish devil brandishing a large . . . *spork,* by the looks of it. Just above the demon was a creepy sign made of doll parts. Plastic arms and legs spelled out UNWELCOME AREA.

Just beyond the kiddie pool landing pad was a little wooden stage, above which hung a sign that said ABANDON ALL HOPE, YE WHO ENTER HERE (AS WELL AS ALL CAMERAS AND ELECTRONIC RECORDING DEVICES). As Milton and Marlo watched, several lizards in gold lamé suits slithered onto the stage. They crawled over busted toy pianos, horns, drums, and guitars and began to plunk, blow, pound, and strum, respectively. Milton rubbed his eyes in disbelief. A longer-than-average lizard sporting Ray-Bans slinked into the spotlight and tapped a tiny microphone.

"Hello? HELLO? Is this thing on? Wow, the sound here is terrible . . . too much *gecko*! I kid . . . A one, two, three, FOUR!"

The band attacked their instruments—twanging, plunking, and bashing out fractured jazz. The lead lizard swung his microphone like a lasso, then brought it to his mouth.

"If you've lived a life so bad
  that you drove your parents and teachers mad,
  one day then, perhaps your last,
  you'll have to pay for every disrupted class.
  Deep down beneath your feet where only bad kids go
  is a place where it's always hot weather,
  and you learn that a demon's forever."

The horn players formed a reptilian conga line. The drummer spun his sticks over his head. One stick flew into the air, hitting Milton in the shin. Without missing a beat the lizard pulled off the tail of the nearest saxophone player and used it to perform an explosive drum solo.

"Yes, you guessed, you're down in Heck.
Here all the brats are nervous wrecks.
Nothing to do to save their necks.
It's always detention down in Heck.
Where all the bad kids go . . ."

The band paused briefly, as if musically leaping off a diving board. Then, with a chaotic splash of sound, the lizards attacked their instruments with reptilian fury.

"Down!!"

The lizards bowed to imaginary applause. Milton, a nice boy even when deceased, started to clap. Marlo elbowed him in the ribs.

Suddenly the dense black smoke cleared in one great whoosh. A terrible, grating metal squeak sliced through the cavern as an ornate iron gate decorated with sugared spikes, candied skulls, and barbed licorice labored open roughly forty feet behind the stage. Beyond it were patches of fluorescent light, winking in nervous flickers through the haze from some vast plaza beyond. Even worse than the metal-on-metal screech was the deathly quiet that followed.

A listless group of grubby children gathered inside the gates, gawking mutely at the new arrivals. They scattered in terror as a sharp clack of hooves broke the silence. A squat, puffy old creature strutted toward Milton and Marlo.

The creature's feet were shiny cloven hooves with gleaming, diamond-studded buckles. The legs atop these fancy hooves were like those of a fat, scabby goat. Above, mounds of scaly flesh were stuffed inside a filthy muumuu, cinched tight by a slithering snakeskin belt— with the snake still inside. Worst of all was its face—*her* face—a lumpy leather avalanche with a mouth rimmed in blood-red lipstick and fiendish scratches that served as eyes. She looked kind of like one of those bullfrogs that swells up, except this particular one had forgotten to swell down.

She stopped just inside the gates, her gruesome face impossible to read. Between her hooves poked the nose—three, actually—of an overly groomed Pekingese with a little something extra in the head department. Three pink bows encircled its three necks. It sniffed the air and growled a malicious three-part harmony.

Milton gulped hard. Even the impossible-to-faze Marlo fidgeted in her vintage granny boots. Marlo looked at her trembling brother. "I don't think we're in Kansas anymore."

The female creature beckoned the children forward with a curl of her long, manicured claws. Marlo and Milton traded anxious glances, then marched beneath the arm of another red plastic devil. Above the devil was a sign that read YOU MUST BE THIS SHORT TO ENTER HECK.

They stepped through the open gates and into a sprawling warehouse of sorts with a low, oppressive ceiling and dirty beige walls. The floor of the warehouse was covered with stained gray carpet that smelled like cat pee and instant soup mix. The carpet was striped with clear plastic runners, apparently to keep the floor from getting any dirtier, though Milton couldn't see how that was possible. Scattered piles of broken toys, broken bottles, and sniveling children with broken spirits were strewn across the facility with no rhyme or reason. The whole place was like a drab, endless day-care center. It oozed tedium and cold despair.

The woman/creature/whatever smiled sweetly, showing several rows of rotten yellow fangs. Behind her the gates began to squeal to a close.

"I am Bea 'Elsa' Bubb. Welcome to Heck," she hissed. "Population: Infinity . . ."

Two bells tolled loudly as the gate clanged shut.

". . . plus two."

3 · iN BEA'S HiVE

MARLO AND MILTON sat on a crinkly floral-patterned couch covered with plastic. Bea "Elsa" Bubb's office and its owner both exuded a distinctive odor: part mothballs, part rose water, part disinfectant, part sour milk, part menthol rub, with a sharp undercurrent somewhere between vomit and neglected cat box.

On the wall were three posters. The first was of a mangy, one-eared cat hanging from a cactus, perched over a roaring fire. The caption read "Why hang in there?" The next showed a mother scorpion scuttling for safety beneath a desert stone. Slimy white larval babies nestled on her back: "Go crawl under a rock." The last was a watercolor cartoon of a man being fit for a noose atop a rickety gallows: "Today is the last day of the rest of your life."

Across from Marlo and Milton was a massive

mahogany desk, ornately carved with demons and smiling clowns with large, moist eyes. Atop the desk was a marble, tombstone-shaped nameplate with BEA "ELSA" BUBB, PRINCIPAL OF DARKNESS etched in Gothic letters.

The pudgy demoness sat behind her desk, her dog in her lap. She stroked one of its heads. Another head cleaned a paw while the remaining one growled suspiciously.

"Now, now, Cerberus," she cooed. "They always smell like that at first."

Milton nervously cleared his throat. "So is this . . . you know . . . he—?"

Principal Bubb shook her swollen claw at Milton. "There will be none of that potty mouth down here. Of course this isn't . . . *that place.* You're in Heck."

Marlo leaned forward, her brow knit. "Heck? What the . . ."

Bea "Elsa" Bubb glowered. Her eyes—inky black pupils adrift in a pus-yellow sea—glowed like fanned embers.

". . . *heck,*" Marlo faltered, "is *Heck*?"

Bea "Elsa" Bubb smiled coldly and clasped her claws together.

"Rather like an *h-e-double-hockey-sticks* for children," she said. "Heck is where the souls of the darned toil for all eternity—or until they turn eighteen, whichever comes first."

Marlo and Milton absentmindedly locked hands. They noticed that they were actually (*eww*) touching and instantly let go.

Milton swallowed. "Um, how do we turn eighteen if we're, you know, dead?"

Principal Bubb rolled her eyes, the vertical gashes of her pupils settling on a stain on the ceiling that resembled dried puke.

"Have you ever heard of the term 'old soul,' dearie?" she asked rhetorically. "Just because we leave the disgusting meat of our former selves up on the Stage . . ."

Milton and Marlo furrowed their eyebrows.

"*The Surface*," Bea "Elsa" Bubb repeated slowly, as if she were talking to a banana slug with a learning disability. "We cast those gauche earthly vehicles aside and our souls move on . . . like a snake shedding its skin. The soul inside us continues to age. And, like you awful children, young souls aren't fully accountable for what they have done—*yet*. Though if I had my way . . ."

Bea "Elsa" Bubb seemed lost in dark, secret thoughts. "Anyway," she said, shaking her head. An earwig tumbled out of one of her pointed ears. "The bleeding hearts upstairs have created this cozy little place for despicable little brats such as yourselves to be rehabilitated and punished—*mostly punished*—so that when your souls reach maturity, they can be judged and sentenced to the full extent of the law. Your ultimate fate is not decided yet, though if you start out here, your everlasting prospects are grim."

Cerberus sniffed the air. His heads growled. Principal Bubb stroked his back.

"What is it, Cerberus sweetie? Did the rat pâté disagree with you?"

The principal inhaled deeply. "Is someone making s'mores?"

Marlo hungrily eyed a glob of burnt marshmallow glued to her bangs, pulled it off, and popped it into her mouth.

"What hap-happens after that?" Milton stammered, aghast.

Bea "Elsa" Bubb sighed like an ancient bellows. She reached for her top drawer and pulled out two bright purple gelatinous candies.

"Here," the principal said, doling out the candies to the children. "Have some Gummo Badgers."

The children eyed the candies. With razor-sharp teeth and claws meticulously sculpted from corn syrup, the candies resembled their vicious, beady-eyed namesakes but looked far more delectable. Ignoring all cautions about taking candy from strangers—and Bea "Elsa" Bubb was about as strange as they came—the two ravenous children snatched the treats and popped them into their mouths.

Not bad, Milton thought. Kind of like marmalade, with just the slightest soaplike aftertaste, but Milton was so hungry he couldn't afford to be picky. After the first few chomps another unwanted effect became evident: Milton's—and Marlo's—mouths were soon cemented shut.

The ancient demoness leaned close and smirked. "That's better," she hissed with breath reeking of old coffee and rotten cavities. "Now sit back, shut up, and I'll give you the official spiel. Maybe I'll even be able to catch my favorite show."

She scratched her back against her chair.

"Anyway," she said, grimacing, "just like up there, you'll be going to school, except the stakes are a little higher . . . or more likely lower in your case. Each soul year you'll be given your SATs—Soul Aptitude Tests. Based on these rigorous, highly standardized exams, your eternal fate will be decided. On graduation day you'll be given your dysploma, thus dissolving our unfortunate relationship. Isn't that nice?"

Milton and Marlo struggled to answer, but all they managed were a few muffled grunts.

Principal Bubb straightened a stack of tattered yellowed papers on her desk, shoved them aside, and set a mummified monkey's paw on top of the pile as a paperweight.

"You're in Limbo now," she said tartly, "the first of the Nine Circles of Heck. The others are Rapacia, Blimpo, Fibble, Snivel, Precocia, Lipptor, Sadia, and Dupli-City. Limbo is smack dab in the middle of the No Time Zone, meaning that timewise, there is no meaning, if you take my meaning. Think of it as detention, where you've got all the time under the world to mull over your new situation, to really think about why you're here—"

Why *are* we here? Milton tried to interject, but it came out more like "Wmm *ahhh* whu heh?"

"Shhhh," the principal hissed dismissively, before continuing with a speech she seemed to know by heart—if she'd *had* a heart, that is. "Hours, minutes, seconds . . . *millenniums* . . . fail to pass. Not even souls age here, which is why I don't look a century past 2,900."

Bea "Elsa" Bubb absentmindedly preened at her grotesque reflection in a burnished-bronze skull cup on her desk. Marlo gagged softly. There was something deeply nauseating about this creature, which resembled a swollen sack of tarantulas, thinking that by smoothing down a row of sprouted wart hairs she was somehow "prettying up."

"You'll still attend classes, of course, but they're more to familiarize yourself with how things work here than anything else," the demoness continued. "For the time being, you are in Limbo, where time has no meaning, and where all newbies go until we sort out exactly which circle of Heck they'll ultimately be assigned to. Every case has to go through our Department of Unendurable Redundancy, Bureaucracy, and Redundancy and they are notoriously, shall we say, *thorough,* so expect a bit of a wait."

Milton stood up, trembling with indignation. He forced his lips free from their Gummo Badger prison. "I don't understand!" he shouted. "I can see why my sister's here . . ."

Marlo shot her brother a dirty look as bright purple drool trickled from the corner of her mouth.

"But I'm a straight-A student!" Milton yelped. "A Boy Scout! Chess Club legend! I take piano lessons! I brush my teeth after every—"

Bea "Elsa" Bubb rose and leaned into Milton's face. "You're a thief," she hissed with a flick of her forked tongue. "And use your inside voice, please."

"*A thief!?*" Milton was outraged. "But I never . . ." He looked at Marlo, who was smirking on the couch.

Milton's eyes bugged. "So I'm facing eternal . . . *darnation* . . . for a tube of kiwi-cantaloupe lip gloss?"

Marlo managed a chuckle through her candy-sealed mouth.

"She tricked me!" Milton yelped. "I didn't know I was stealing! This is unfair!"

Bea "Elsa" Bubb clapped her claws together with a dry, leathery slap.

Instantly she, her desk, and the children were hurled backward through a long, stone tunnel.

4 · LAIR OF THE LIAR

MILTON, MARLO, AND Bea "Elsa" Bubb plunged into a dark, high-tech lair of security screens, blinking computers, and a long electronic Netherworld Soul Exchange (NSE) ticker scrolling gibberish and numbers.

Principal Bubb rose from her chair and clacked toward an immense filing cabinet adorned with padlocks. She extended a long rigid nail cut into intricate notches and fit it inside one of the locks. With a twist she opened the lock and pulled out two files from the drawer.

The two files were not created equal. In fact, if both were placed on the scales of justice, one would have catapulted the other straight up to the Galactic Order Department headquarters.

Bea "Elsa" Bubb tossed the files on her desk, plopped back down into her seat, and opened the first, which was crammed with papers.

"Marlo Fauster," she said, flipping through the count-less infractions. "An open-and-shut case."

Marlo grinned with pride.

Principal Bubb opened the other file. It was empty save for a Post-it note.

"And Milton Fauster." She chuckled. "This is pa-thetic."

Written on the Post-it were the following words:

> one act of petty larceny
> just before departure.

Bea "Elsa" Bubb's snicker trailed away. This was the sorriest excuse for a sin she had ever seen. It struck her as some kind of a mistake, except that making a mis-take here was a mistake never made. Heck had run as a faultlessly foul machine for longer than anyone could remember . . . before memory, even. Principal Bubb wasn't about to let some ghastly goody-goody undo all she had worked so hard to uphold down here.

Milton was quivering with righteous anger. "I didn't do it! My sister's the evil one! Just ask anybody!"

Cerberus, coiled beneath Bea "Elsa" Bubb's hooves like a furry, three-headed cobra, looked up at Milton's outburst. The ancient demoness put Operation Cover-up into motion.

"The devil's in the details," she said coolly, opening her top drawer and pulling out a large remote control.

It was a real beauty, with more blinking buttons than a blinking-button factory. She waved it at a wall of screens, and the cavern exploded with noise and light. Marlo and Milton covered their ears as grainy video footage streamed across the massive screens.

Marlo, as seen from a department store security camera, examines several large bottles of perfume: Siren's Song ("Drive Him to His Doom"), Aroma Borealis, and Scentless Tragedy. She scoots like a crab down the counter, fingering tubes of lipstick and mascara. Suddenly Marlo yells and points toward the other side of the store. The heavily made-up shop girl pivots her head in the same direction. In the blink of an eye Marlo grabs a fistful of expensive cosmetics and drops them off the edge of the screen into a makeup bag. The motion freezes while the camera zooms in on Milton's blurry self, cradling the bag and staring obliviously off into space.

Bea "Elsa" Bubb snapped off the TVs. Milton put his head in his hands and moaned. "I don't get it," he said. "One little crime puts me away with Miss Demeanor over here . . ."

Bea "Elsa" Bubb folded her arms together and glared at Milton.

"The Big Guy Upstairs doesn't grade on a curve," she said. "While you may have frittered away the majority of your young life being a good little sheep up on the Stage, as you can plainly see now, it was all for naught.

"Your last sin is typically your greatest," Principal Bubb continued. "Your act of thievery—whether intentional or not—counted so heavily because it was your very last, with no chance to redeem yourself before your sticky end."

She shifted her weight from one buttock to another, and possibly a third. "Up there, it's all about first impressions. Here, it's all about your last."

The lumpy lizard-like demoness put her hooves up on her desk. "Do you have any idea how many souls are upstairs in the penthouse?"

Marlo and Milton traded a glance.

"Go on. Hazard a guess," Principal Bubb dared.

Marlo finally wrenched her mouth free of the sticky Gummo Badger candy.

"A million?" Marlo ventured, her lips feeling like they had been injected with Novocain. "A *billion*?"

Bea "Elsa" Bubb's eyes crinkled with cold amusement. "Not even warm . . . and it's always warm here. Try *seventeen*."

Marlo's and Milton's jaws practically dropped to the stone floor.

"Yes," she continued. "Of all the humans throughout history, only seventeen made the cut."

Marlo leaned forward with a look of utter disbelief. "George Washington?"

"Ah, yes, who could never tell a lie," Bea "Elsa" Bubb spat back. "But he seemed to have no problem owning slaves and leading thousands to war."

"Joan of Arc?" Milton chimed in.

"French," she answered.

"Mother Theresa?" Marlo asked.

"She once had the gall to take a day off after contracting dysentery."

Milton shook his head. "Of all the things that don't make sense here, that makes the least."

Principal Bubb sneered. "I don't expect your just-dead brains to understand the nuances of our afterlife system. Your heads are still warm with how things *were*. But you'll have plenty of time to understand how things work, believe me.

"Suffice it to say that there is a just reward for all creatures, great and not so great. Mother Theresa is enjoying a perfectly acceptable hereafter. It's just that the deluxe afterlife suite with all the divine trimmings is reserved for a select few. Her accommodations in Sixth Heaven are comfortable and near beatific, merely without the lavish frills and exclusive privileges, and with only limited access to the main grounds. But the buffet, I hear, is to die for."

She settled back into her plush velveteen rabbit–upholstered chair, scooted closer to her desk, and pulled out two long pieces of parchment paper from her top drawer.

"As much as I'm enjoying our little chat," Principal Bubb said coolly, "we must get back to business."

She placed two lengthy contracts before them. "I just need your grubby signatures here and here," she said as her claws scraped the paper.

Milton leaned over the contract, scrutinizing it through his one good lens.

𝕿𝖍𝖎𝖘 𝕴𝖓𝖉𝖊𝖓𝖙𝖚𝖗𝖊,

by and between Heck, a branch of the Galactic Order Department, itself an independent offshoot of the Cosmic Omnipotence and Regulation Entity, hereinafter, whether singular or plural, masculine, feminine, neuter, terrestrial, extraterrestrial, and/or interdimensional, designated as "Soul Holder," which expression shall include Soul Holder's executors, administrators, assigns, and successors in interest, and Milton Fauster, hereinafter, designated as "Soul Relinquisher," witnesseth this legally binding covenant.

Milton's eyes were as glazed as doughnuts.

Principal Bubb handed them two long, black glistening pens.

Milton and Marlo gulped as one and reluctantly took the strangely soft pens. The instant their fingers wrapped around them, two small serpent heads emerged from either end. One end of each sunk its fangs into the forearms of the siblings. Milton and Marlo screamed as the pens drew blood. The heads at the far end of each "pen" grinned widely and reached toward the contract, signing Milton's and Marlo's names in bright, wet crimson.

As soon as the signatures were drawn, the snakes uncoiled and slithered out of the children's hands and back into Principal Bubb's top drawer. Clutching their throbbing arms, Milton and Marlo sniffed back tears. Bea "Elsa" Bubb took the contracts and with a wave of her claw, conjured two copies out of thin air. The principal clacked over to her file cabinet and tucked all four documents away.

"There . . . signed, sealed, and delivered," she said with a cackle. "You are now officially mine in every possible way—and a few impossible ways—for all eternity, or until you turn eighteen, blah blah blah . . ."

Milton and Marlo wept silently.

"Now, now," she said as she sat back down in her chair. "I can't stand to see young people cry . . . So go away. We're done here."

Milton and Marlo stared at each other through blurry eyes, baffled. Principal Bubb, ignoring the two children as if they had suddenly ceased to exist, pulled a dark chocolate, double-fudge, triple-nougat, quadruple-caramel, peanut-butter candy bar from her bottom drawer and took a massive bite. Gooey strands of pure deliciousness hung from her fangs. Despite their new-found distrust of Heck candy, the two siblings gasped with unconcealed desire. Dying sure gave one a hearty appetite.

"Hungry?" she asked with mock sweetness, like a diet soda. "Go to the cafeterium down the hall, stuff your repugnant little faces, and await your official disorientation."

Cerberus yapped and leapt back into her lap. One of his heads (the least hideous one) licked Bea's pointy, leathery ear.

"What's that, sweetums?" she cooed. Cerberus whimpered softly. "Oh, that's right! It's time for our show!"

Bea "Elsa" Bubb jiggled the remote and brought all of the screens back to life. Each featured the same image: a pitchfork against a backdrop of fiery brimstone. Beneath, in drippy red letters, read URN: THE UNDERWORLD RETRIBUTION NETWORK. The image dissolved in a curtain of pure flame.

The show's announcer bellowed with a voice like a rusty foghorn: "Here he is, the Dark Angel you love to hate (and hate to admit you love), Mephistopheles, the Lord of Darkness, call him what thou wilt, just don't call him late to Revelation . . . Ladies, gentlemen, and lesser demons, give it up for Luuuuuuuucifer!!"

Milton and Marlo looked at each other and shrugged. Milton noticed an exit nestled between two banks of filing cabinets. He smacked his sister on the shoulder (which was easy considering he was still mad at her), and the two siblings crept across Principal Bubb's lair, leaving her to ogle with glazed goo-goo eyes the supremely evil object of her affection, that devilishly handsome hunk of Hades: the Big Guy Downstairs.

5 · THE NOT-SO-GREAT ESCAPE

MILTON AND MARLO walked cautiously down the hallway that would, in theory, lead them to the cafeterium. The winding, uneven passageway smelled like a hospital, full of that ammonia, rubbing alcohol, and sickness reek that stung your eyes and sunk your spirits.

Yet instead of a place to eat, Milton and Marlo emerged into a cluttered, indoor playground—a FOUL PLAYGROUND, if the faltering neon sign was to be believed.

Warped hula hoops, two-wheeled tricycles, deflated basketballs, not-so-Hot Wheels, well-mannered Bratz, way-too Raggedy Anns, powerless Game Boys, ex-Xboxes, and an astounding collection of Russian poetry lay scattered across the dingy gray carpet. Pressed close above was a crumbling checkerboard of asbestos tiles and glaring fluorescent light fixtures.

Milton and Marlo passed through waves of depressed children. It was like they had stumbled upon a Disneyland for the doomed, the unhappiest place on earth, though they were miles below earth . . . or to the side of it . . . or wherever. Milton still wasn't sure if he was anywhere at all. All he knew was that he, or the person he used to be, or the person he thought he used to be, was hungry. Did he still have a stomach? Did he really need to eat? Or was appetite simply some ingrained habit, like his compulsive nail biting and unrelenting need to brush exactly one hundred times after each meal?

"Unholy moly." Marlo snickered. "Get a load of that!"

With her shiny black fingernail Marlo pointed toward a group of large shaggy creatures lumbering into the foul playground and scooping up the younger children in their arms. The toddlers wriggled and screamed. The creatures were obviously, to Milton's eleven-year-old eyes, simply people in costumes—thick greenish fur that looked like glowing, overgrown tree moss, spiny orange horns, one big red glowing eye, and rows of plastic yellow teeth. They weren't even particularly scary costumes, but they were frightening enough to soil the Underoos of Heck's younger unfortunates.

Marlo chuckled. "What's that getup supposed to be, anyway? A Boogeyman or something?"

One of the costumed creatures stopped and removed its head.

"That's Boogey*person*," hissed a hideous, decomposing demon with goopy yellow eyes, a moist snout, and lipsticked lips covered with cold sores.

The creature resecured its head and shambled after its fellow Boogeypeople.

Milton and Marlo quivered with fear.

"Wow," Marlo managed between chattering teeth. "Lucky for the runts those super-freaky gross things are in disguise . . . Now where the heck are we? I'm so hungry I could eat a horse with a side of ponies."

The Boogeypeople dragged the terrified toddlers to a large room with glass walls on the edge of the foul playground. Above the sliding glass door was a rusty sign caked with peeling lead paint: KINDERSCARE: WHERE LITTLE KIDS GET BIG NIGHTMARES. Inside there was a haggard teacher, with claw marks on her face and a few jagged bites taken out of her midsection, putting several weeping tykes down for their naps in coffins made of gingerbread. The teacher limped to the door and flipped over a sign that read: BEWARE: KID NAPPING IN PROGRESS.

Marlo stared at the sign while rubbing her chin. Milton tugged on her singed velvet skirt.

"Look, over here."

Milton led his sister to an illuminated map beyond the KinderScare facility and the Unwelcome Area, just inside the Gates of Heck.

"Hmmm . . ." Marlo muttered as she traced her finger from the blinking red You Are Here dot on the map to the cafeterium, an oval blob that connected to a room labeled "Disorientation Center." "That's weird," she continued. "Everything below the Disorientation Center is grayed out." Indeed, the semicircle—half of the subterranean campus of Limbo—was "censored" with an obnoxious little label plastered over the gray: "Wouldn't You Like to Know?!"

Behind the KinderScare facility was the infirmary and, just beyond, a bright square indicating Bea "Elsa" Bubb's office. Behind it was a long rectangle marked "Principal Bubb's Secret Lair."

Marlo straightened suddenly. "I've got an idea."

Milton's phantom stomach stopped, dropped, and rolled. "Don't you think that maybe you've had enough brilliant ideas for one day?" Milton posed as tactfully as possible. "Perhaps we should just relax and, you know, assess our situation. How about that?"

"What?" Marlo glowered, her china doll–like face creased with a sour look of someone at least three times her age. "You don't think I can get us out of here? That just because I'm not a little book maggot like you, I don't have the smarts to plot an escape? Me, who managed to steal the entire window display at Dullard's not once but *five* times without being caught?"

Milton sighed. He was doomed.

"Didn't one of your great ideas put us here in the first place?" he asked.

Marlo looked over her shoulder toward the Kinder-Scare facility.

"Like I could have known a marshmallow bear would pack that much explosive power. There should really be a law against—"

"Against shoplifting and fooling your little brother into becoming an accessory?" Milton interjected.

Marlo leaned down to Milton and pinched his cheek. Then she smoothed out her dress and placed her hand between his shoulder blades, where Milton more than likely would have sprouted wings someday if his sister hadn't screwed up his life everlasting.

"Really, it's a good plan," Marlo stated with conviction. "Besides, if it doesn't work, what are they going to do, extra-double-with-chocolate-jimmies-sprinkled-on-top punish us?"

They made their way toward KinderScare and peered through a window made blurry with filthy handprints and goopy snot smears. Rows of fussy porcelain knickknacks and potpourri bowls sat on mantelpieces lining the peeling walls—walls that were covered with patches of mildew.

Most of the toddlers were pretending to be asleep in their frosted gingerbread coffins. Some were clutching each other, screaming as Boogeypeople read them alternating selections from Edgar Allan Poe's "The Tell-Tale Heart" and Danielle Steel's *Toxic Bachelors*. A small group of sickly preschoolers with dark circles under their eyes trembled in a corner, trying to kick their addiction to phonics.

"Remember," Marlo said, glancing over her shoulder as she approached the KinderScare facility, "follow my lead."

Milton could only imagine where that lead would lead to.

Marlo burst into the room. The Boogeypeople on duty looked at the door, like owls at the sight of a scurrying rodent.

Marlo noticed a sullen child with a mop of matted black hair. The eyes were wrong, she thought, but it would have to do.

"My precious baby!" Marlo squealed hysterically as she rushed toward the child. "Your loving mother is here to right the terrible wrong that has been done to us!"

She scooped the wriggling child into her arms.

"You not my mama," the child protested in a grating whine that even a *real* mother would have had trouble loving.

Marlo covered the little brat's mouth and squeezed the child tightly to her chest while Milton hovered in the doorway.

"There, there, my little miracle," she cooed as the

child—who smelled like cooked cabbage—struggled in her arms. "It's all right to be confused. No child should have to go through what you went through, my sweet bundle of angel giggles."

The Boogeyperson in charge took off its shaggy green head, exposing the wretched beast within. Children screamed and backed away desperately.

"What is going on here?" the reptilian demon hissed.

Marlo held up her head defiantly. "I am here for my baby. Nothing can come between a mother and her son—"

"Daughter," the creature countered. Behind the creature, a small sandy-haired boy sidled toward a locked chest.

"Whatever," Marlo continued. "I'm highly distraught. The point is that family ties can never be severed."

Milton, still in the doorway, silently wished that they could at least be stretched.

The Boogeyperson scrutinized Marlo. Without even turning its disgusting head, it swatted the sandy-haired boy away from the chest.

"I told you, Julius," the creature said, "you cannot have your things. They are only there in the chest to torment you."

"B-b-b-ut," the boy stuttered with flecks of spittle on his cracked lips, his eyes wild, "m-m-my flash cards . . . m-m-my . . . *phonics* . . ."

"Go play Duck, Duck, Noose with the other children," the Boogeyperson said, never taking its hot, beady eyes off Marlo. "Aren't you a little young to be someone's mother?"

Marlo looked back at Milton expectantly. He drew a weary breath and shambled into KinderScare.

"Um," stammered Milton, "she—my sister—is rather old for her age. She comes from a broken home and has made a lot of really stupid decisions in her life. *Incredibly stupid.* I mean, it's surprising to think a human brain was actually involved in some of the idiotic things—"

"Thank you, dear brother," Marlo said with a cold glare. "I think the Boogeyman gets the point."

"Boogey*person*!" the creature spat.

"Ou smell funny," the fidgety child mumbled from behind Marlo's hand. "Like a s'more."

"You're so cute I could just squeeze the life out of you," Marlo said.

Another Boogeyperson joined its supervisor, removing its head to a second chorus of young shrieks.

"So how did your 'bundle of angel giggles' get here, anyhow?" the demonic day-care worker asked skeptically.

Marlo smoothed down the child's hair as it tried to swat her hand away. "Um . . . running around a swimming pool . . . on a full stomach . . . with scissors."

Marlo cradled the squirming child in her arms and slowly backed away toward the front door.

"And, after drowning my sorrows with a fistful of

Pop Rocks and a pint of extra-fizzy ginger ale, I ended up here, on a rescue mission to save my baby."

Marlo trotted quickly out the door, straight to the Gates of Heck, with Milton and the Boogeypeople close behind.

"Put me down, koo-koo pants!" the child whined like a dentist's drill.

Soon the foul playground was full of children, demons, and Boogeypeople alike, all gawking at Marlo as she raised the twisting tot above her head.

"Attention, freaky creatures of Heck!" Marlo bellowed. The growing throng of agitated onlookers pressed Milton close to his sister. "Open this gate so me and my son—"

"Daughter!" yelled several Boogeypeople.

"Whatever! Open this gate now or else I will be forced to do something . . . something really bad. Something only a grief-crazed mother would do . . ."

The demons pressed closer. The surrounding mob and the queasy feeling in Milton's stomach gave him a profound sense of déjà vu, as if he were right back up at the mall. But could you really have déjà vu for something that had only just happened?

Marlo's eyes grew wide. "Help me out here," she murmured from the corner of her mouth.

"I will if you admit you have a knack for hatching really stupid plans . . ."

"Sure . . ."

". . . and I'm complimenting you by even consider-ing them 'plans' . . ."

"All right already!"

Milton swallowed and stepped forward.

"Demons, caregivers, despondent children . . . I be-seech thee. Do not judge my emotionally unstable sis-ter by her actions. Judge her instead by the savage injustice of her situation."

The agitated horde of demons calmed somewhat.

"Imagine, if you will, that the one thing that meant anything to you at all was suddenly taken from you in a senseless tragedy. Imagine the lengths you would go to retrieve that which was stolen from you."

A Boogeyperson wiped a tear from its eye.

"So please," Milton said with a dramatic sweep of his arms. "Let us go free before a tortured mother is forced to do the unspeakable . . . hurt the very thing she loves the most in this and all worlds."

Unbeknownst to the Fausters, a fuzzy white head poked out of Milton's backpack. Lucky sniffed yet an-other outraged mob and had his own furry bout of déjà vu. He bared his teeth.

The crowd backed away a step. Milton and Marlo gaped at each other.

"Wow, runt," Marlo whispered. "You certainly have a way with words. I should have exploited that more fully when we were alive."

Just then a bell tolled, and the Gates of Heck slowly

creaked open. Puffs of smoke gusted into the Unwelcome Area. The child in Marlo's arms took the opportunity to bite her captor's hand, struggle to the floor, and wriggle away.

"Oww!" Marlo yelped, clutching her torn lace sleeve. "You ungrateful little son of a—!"

"Daughter!" barked a Boogeyperson at the front of the tense crowd, snatching up the child.

"Whatever," mumbled Marlo as she turned toward the opening gates.

"If you've lived a life so bad,
  that you drove your parents and teachers mad . . ."

"Not again!" whined a little red-haired boy near the gate, clapping his hands over his ears. The lounge lizards had again taken to their tiny stage. *What a miserable gig,* Milton thought.

"Where all the bad kids go.
  Down . . ."

The smoke cleared. Out limped a dark smudge of a boy. A cruel boy. A boy all too familiar to Milton. A boy whose name was *still* Damian.

With bandages wrapped around his head and a cast on his leg, Damian emerged from the cloud like a brawny mummy.

Milton's jaw dropped open. "Oh my God . . ."

"I doubt if he can hear you," Marlo said, rubbing her hand.

Damian hobbled through the crowd, which parted for him in realization that Heck had a new alpha bully. Damian grinned a rotten, snaggletoothed grin at his new subjects. Where others saw only broken toys and brimstone, Damian saw opportunity.

"Cool!" he snorted.

Damian then caught sight of the Fausters. His face became a mask of amused malevolence.

"Well, well. If it isn't little Milquetoast, the four-eyed freak."

As Damian the mummy limped closer, Marlo said to Milton, "Is this that bully you're always talking about, the one with a little something extra in the chromosome department?"

"Zip it, corpse bride," Damian spat.

Milton shook his head in total bewilderment. "How did you get here? I mean, I know why—obviously—as you're a terrible, terrible person, but . . ."

"Well, after the . . . *incident*," Damian said while absentmindedly twirling one of the soiled bandages unraveling from his head, "which *ruled,* by the way, I was taken to the hospital and hooked up to a machine. Some idiot tripped on the cord and unplugged me. It's all a little hazy. I think I saw a gigantic stick of butter holding a balloon that said "Get Butter Soon!" Or maybe it was just my stepuncle. That stingy jerk."

Suddenly it hit Milton like two thousand pounds of rectangular clay blocks. Marlo may have been to blame for *where* he ended up, but Damian was responsible for *why*.

"If it weren't for you," he fumed, "I'd be home studying!!!"

Milton lunged at Damian, his noodle arms swinging wildly. Unfortunately, for every one of Milton's noodle smacks, Damian delivered two beefy blows, and soon Milton's face began to resemble a plate of spaghetti with extra marinara sauce.

Marlo looked over at a pair of leathery demon guards with batlike wings who were watching the scuffle and snickering. She had to think fast, as her brother's face was beginning to look like a swelling relief map of Bruisetonia.

Marlo rushed toward her brother's hulking foe and . . . *kissed him* . . . on the lips, on his chunky, filthy cheeks, and on his barely perceptible neck. Then she wrapped her spindly white arms around him (as much as she could) and gave him a big, warm, and—for all appearances—sincere squeeze.

Damian was momentarily paralyzed by this—or any—public display of affection. The demon guards, however, were quick to act.

"Stop that this instant!" croaked the taller of the two guards. The two twisted hunks of living jerky swooped in to break up the spontaneous love fest.

As the guards pried the children apart, Marlo grabbed Milton.

"My . . . face . . . ," Milton mumbled behind bubbles of blood and spit. "It has a pulse."

Marlo helped him up onto his shaky legs while the demon guards restrained Damian. "Cool off, lover boy," one of them hissed.

The crowd grew quiet. Too quiet. Like when a school of little fish disappears just before a shark makes a surprise visit.

The sound of hooves filled the Unwelcome Area.

"My, my," Bea "Elsa" Bubb murmured, standing before Damian with a look bordering on reverence.

"Damian Ruffino. What an honor to have you darkening our humble halls."

She extended her claw. As Damian stared at her obsessively manicured talons, the principal shot a sharp, information-packed look at the demon guards holding him. They quickly released Damian, who shrugged off their grasp with an angry shake.

A smirk crossed his face as the situation slowly dawned on him—and with Damian, just about every dawn rose slowly. He reached out his hand to Principal Bubb, then, just before contact, pulled it back and smoothed his hair. The ancient demoness grinned.

"You have quite the following down here," she said, lowering her claw to her side. "We could learn a lot from a self-starting, energetic, creative yet thuggishly primitive go-getter such as yourself."

Principal Bubb placed her sharp, scaly hand on Damian's back. "I'm sure we'll be best fiends."

Damian sharpened his cruel eyes into glaring slits as he strutted past Milton and Marlo on his way to Bea "Elsa" Bubb's not-so-secret lair.

"Let's get you something to eat," Marlo said to Milton. "That's what we were trying to do anyway, right?"

"As long as it's not a knuckle sandwich," gurgled Milton as he and his sister hobbled down the hallway. "I think I've had plenty for one day."

6 · AN UNHAPPY MEAL WiTH A SiDE OF FUZZ

MILTON AND MARLO entered the dreary cafeterium. A small group of kids was staring up at an ancient flickering television bolted in the corner. The children sat slumped over plates filled with runny lumps that oozed over the edges. They looked from the warped black-and-white picture on the screen to each other, as if unsure whether they were awake or dead to the world. Or both.

On the screen the show's title, *I Love Lucifer*, was branded upon a writhing demon's back.

"Bad evening, ladies and virulent germs!" the show's star said with a devilish grin. His dashing tail swayed with confidence as he waved to the crowd like a game-show emcee.

In one corner of the cafeterium, beneath a banner proclaiming "Unwelcome, Class of Now," stood a row of Automat vending machines. Behind dozens of little glass doors was a selection of unappetizing foodstuffs—plates of quivering Jell-O hiding pineapple, cherry, and olive chunks; strange gray sandwiches sealed in plastic; and slabs of dry, mysterious meats that bore no resemblance to the animals from whence they supposedly came.

Some of the compartments, however, contained mouthwatering morsels, the likes of which Milton and Marlo had never seen. Exotic pizzas with layers of savory toppings; yard-long hot dogs slathered with ketchup, mustard, chili, bacon, and gravy; and hot fudge sundaes on glazed Krispy Kreme bowls, topped with shredded candy bars. These special compartments were easy to spot, since they were the ones with hands of screaming boys and girls trapped in their doors.

Milton watched a pudgy, freckle-faced boy walk down the aisle of squealing tykes. The boy was entranced by a triple-decker fudge brownie. He licked his lips and pried open the door. It slammed shut just as the boy's fingers touched the decadent treat. He groaned in anguish like a wounded bear.

Milton edged away from the tempting, baited machine toward the buffet.

"Go get us a table," Milton said. "I'll be fine."

Marlo gave her brother a look of sisterly concern—

a typical sister that didn't trick her little brother into stealing, thus darning his soul for all eternity—then shrugged her shoulders and walked away. Milton grabbed a rusty metal tray and slid it past buckets of steaming Brussels sprouts so overcooked that they resembled wilted globs of pale green snot.

A gruesome female demon manned the buckets of sour-smelling slop. She sported a series of hairy moles and weeping boils and wore a hairnet over her bald head.

She ladled food onto Milton's dirty plate. Milton eyed his mound of Brussels sprouts.

"Excuse me," Milton asked politely. "Might there be anything else besides . . . whatever these are. Certain vegetables, unless they are organic, tend to wreak havoc on my gastrointestinal . . ."

The cafeterium demon stared at Milton with the cold, blank gaze of yesterday's catch of the day.

"You mean like pepperoni pizza?" she rasped. "Turkey with all the trimmings? Fried chicken, mashed potatoes, and gravy? Triple cheeseburgers with chili fries? Hot buffalo wings glistening with honey barbecue sauce?"

Milton nodded enthusiastically.

The cafeterium demon sneered. "No. Just Brussels sprouts."

She glopped another dull splatful onto Milton's plate. The smile slid off his face and landed somewhere at his sneakers. He shuffled away.

Marlo sat alone at a metal table that looked suspiciously like the kind found in a county morgue. She halfheartedly stabbed a couple of slabs of what must at some point have been liver with her fork. Milton slid into the chair beside her.

"Where'd you get that?" he asked with disgust.

She frowned at her plate. "Shock of shocks, from one of the weird food machine thingies that *wasn't* booby-trapped."

She picked up one of the sickening slabs of oily meat and held it out to Milton.

"Here," she said. "This one's yours."

Milton made a face. "I'm not eating that."

"Who said anything about eating it?"

Marlo flung the liver onto Milton's face. He clutched its soothing coolness.

"Oh," he replied meekly. "Thanks."

As the swelling around his left eye and cheek went down somewhat, Milton noticed that his mouth tasted like an old man's T-shirt soaked in sour blood.

"Hey, let me have some of your juice," he said, pointing to a small white juice box next to her plate.

Marlo shrugged her shoulders while Milton took a sip. He spat out the contents in a spray of disgust.

"Ugh! What is that?"

"Cod-liver oil." Marlo smirked.

Milton tried to brush the taste off of his tongue. "Id dat all dey hab?"

"There's sulfur water over there."

Milton got up.

"It's like drinking a fart," Marlo added.

Milton sat back down. He tossed his backpack on the table, put his swollen head in his hands, and cried. "This sucks."

Marlo rolled her eyes and patted her brother on the back. "At least we can finally watch TV while we eat, since Mom's not around."

They stared up at the worst television *ever* to see Lucifer flip his head back and laugh like a scary Pez dispenser. "Phew! Is it hot in here, or is it just me!?"

Milton sobbed weakly at the table. Being dead was bad enough. Being dead and locked away for all eternity with Damian, the bane of his existence—now of his nonexistence—was too terrible for him to even comprehend.

"Maybe this is all just a bad dream," Marlo offered.

"A shared delusion?" Milton sniffed. Even his tear ducts hurt.

"Yeah, like Thanksgiving with Uncle Walter," Marlo said. "But don't worry. With your brains and my . . . *everything else,* we'll come up with some way out of here. We're just getting the lay of the land, is all. We should just relax a bit and, you know, assess our situation."

Milton's backpack rustled. The siblings exchanged disturbed glances. The sack trembled again, as if it was about to give birth to a bag baby. Suddenly out leapt a fuzzy and, to the Fauster children, wonderful animal.

"Lucky!" Milton squealed as he clutched his nervous, wriggling, pink-eyed ferret.

Marlo tickled the animal under the chin. The two red dice hanging from his collar made a tinkling noise.

"If ever there was a more ironically named animal . . . ," cooed Marlo. "Poor guy."

Milton held Lucky close. The ferret gave Milton's wounded face a few loving laps before squirming and hacking up a fur ball.

"This is a sign!" Marlo gasped with wide, spooky eyes. "All we've got to do is stick together!"

Just then the room trembled and went dark. Red strobe lights flashed and an announcement squawked from speakers embedded in the walls.

"Hall demonitors and den mortems, please escort the newly dead to the Disorientation Center immediately."

A row of decomposing demons with badges pinned to their chests filed into the cafeterium and surrounded the trembling children.

A rangy demon with black, papery skin and a runny snout stepped forward.

"Come with us, or Elsa," it hissed.

7 · UNTOGETHER FOREVER

THE NASTY, WIRY little demons herded the children into a long room dimly lit by bare, dangling bulbs. It was difficult for Milton to see how big the room was, as darkness clung to the walls and the slight swaying of the bulbs distorted all perspective.

A thin demon sporting a maggot-ridden meat necktie gestured toward the crowd of confused children.

" *'Where am I, where am I?'* " the creature mocked in a whiny voice. "You're in Heck's Disorientation Center. Now girls on this side, boys on the other," he ordered.

"NO!" screamed Milton as little, grotesquely cute demons wielding pitchsporks shepherded the frightened boys and girls in opposite directions. Marlo's and Milton's eyes locked together. It was strange, thought Milton as he watched his sister being herded away through a curtain of smoke, for most of his life the sight of his sister leaving inspired feelings of great joy. Now, down here in his so-called afterlife, he felt as if a part of him was being ripped away. Having a sister was weird. It was like having a heart-shaped bruise.

The thin demon shuffled in front of the weeping boys, rolling all five of his eyes with exasperation.

"You are experiencing your feelings, which is healthy and normal," he said with condescension. "Now knock it off! I'm Mr. Hecubus, your counselor, and I'd like to officially unwelcome you to Disorientation Day."

Insect-like demons squeezed accordions, filling the center with warped circus music. Strobe lights flashed while slurping noises poured out of bullhorns overhead. The whole effect was indeed quite disorienting.

"Where are the girls going?!" cried Milton.

Mr. Hecubus's eyes trained on Milton. He suddenly felt like a deer caught in five headlights.

"Awww, does we missum the pwetty wittle girls?" Mr. Hecubus mocked. "Well, young pseudoman, don't get your knickers in a bunch. Those representing the fairer sex are going to their very own, specially pH-balanced section of Limbo. Do you want to know why?"

"Why?" asked Milton.

"Cherry pie."

Milton hated falling for that one. Mr. Hecubus smirked.

"The reason is simple: boys and girls have distinct

fears to exploit and different opportunities for humiliation. You will all be allowed to 'mix' again in the future, but only when it is especially degrading and embarrassing."

Mr. Hecubus straightened his putrid meat tie as a squad of little demons scrambled beside him carrying two long flaming poles. They held each pole horizontally at their waists. The sizzling poles stretched out for dozens of feet on either side.

Half of the nauseatingly cute little demons jabbed the boys in their bottoms with shiny pitchsporks, prodding them toward one of the flaming poles. The other half poked the girls toward their own pole on the other side of the Disorientation Center.

Mr. Hecubus threw back his head and cackled. "In the meantime, in-between time, ain't we got fun . . ."

Using their pitchsporks as jaunty canes, the little demons moved their knotty bodies in something resembling a dance. Milton watched Marlo slowly fade into the smoke with all of the other girls. She looked like a pale, weeping ghost. His sister mouthed something to him right before she disappeared. It almost seemed like "I love you, loser," but it was hard to tell.

Milton waved in slow motion. He was too scared to say goodbye. He felt that if he said that, he would never see Marlo again. Instead he yelled, *"Au revoir."* That was French for "until we meet again," which made him feel better, or less worse, anyway.

Milton sighed deeply. He was used to being alone. Milton actually kind of liked it. He could read, daydream . . . whatever he wanted. But he wasn't used to feeling lonely. And as the last shrieking girl vanished into the smog, Milton felt completely abandoned, set adrift in a situation even worse than summer camp. He was so lonely it physically hurt.

"Oww!" he squealed as a pitchspork made unwelcome contact with his bottom.

So Milton and the other petrified boys leaned backward and limboed under the burning pole into Limbo, with twisted carnival music and demon chants egging them on.

"How low can you go? How low can you go?"

8 · CURS AND WEiGH

MILTON'S NORMALLY MOPLIKE hair was singed at the top, giving him a little charred patch that made him look like a monk who had recently escaped a fire. In fact, all the boys looked as if they'd had flaming, limbo-pole haircuts.

Limbo, Milton thought. He vaguely remembered a social studies class on Haiti. His teacher, Mrs. Ryswick, had talked about the limbo dance and how its name was derived from the rite's original purpose. One week after the funeral of a loved one, the mourners would dance under the pole to help the soul of the dearly departed escape the state of Limbo.

Milton and the other boys stumbled, smoldering, through a curtain of smoke into a white corridor.

I guess it doesn't work if you're dancing for your own soul, Milton reflected.

In front of them was a great door ornately carved with slender gods rowing frightened children down a river. It creaked open. Out stepped what seemed like a slender god himself. Draped in a shimmering white tunic, this trim, towering creature was every inch an ancient deity, right from his perfect leather sandals to the tip of his wet dog nose.

"Come with me," the creature barked at Milton, who unfortunately stood at the front of the line.

Milton forced his legs to obey. He followed the creature through the open door and into a massive round chamber of gleaming white marble and gold. Lining the walls were rows and rows of jars filled with squirming black globs sparsely speckled with bright colors. Nine descending rings led down to a stage of pure, polished gold. On the stage was an elaborate scale with two teetering trays. Beneath it was a squat, froglike creature with glistening translucent skin. Milton could see its many internal organs throbbing like pulsating lumps of meat. It resembled one of the horrible Jell-O atrocities chock-full of unfathomable chunks in the cafeterium, only this one was large, alive, and wearing a headset.

The chamber was breathtaking. What struck Milton most was the silence. It was a silence so quiet it was deafening. He could feel its hush whispering all around him in ancient tongues. Milton was in awe. He was standing in a place beyond good and evil, somewhere sacred and old.

Then the jelly creature ripped a wet, explosive fart.

The force of the blast made Milton's ears pop. The smell was like moldy cottage cheese and rotten anchovies wrapped in an old gym sock.

"Aaaaah," the creature sighed with a smile. "That was so big I should give it a name."

The dog god covered its nose with its hands. "Ammit, really. Have you no respect?"

"Oh, go chase a stick, Annubis," Ammit replied while tightening a bolt on the scale.

Milton spoke in groggy tones, as if in a dream. "Where am I? What is this place?"

Annubis smiled, exposing sharp, well-cared-for canine teeth. "You are in the Assessment Chamber, the hallowed halls that hold the Scales of Justice."

The dog god then knelt behind Milton to sniff his bottom. Milton whipped around clutching the back of his pants.

"What are you doing?" Milton squealed.

Annubis rose. "I was simply trying to get to know you."

He smoothed his lustrous tunic with ruffled dignity and continued.

"Here is where your soul is weighed on the primordial scales. A sample is then taken and delivered to our forensics unit, where a series of tests are conducted. They sift through your soul's sediment—the by-product of your moral experiences—and discern exactly where you deserve to spend your eternity."

Annubis took Milton's hand and led him toward the scale. The dog-headed man exuded a strong sense of calm and gentleness.

"The Assessment Chamber is in Limbo," Annubis continued. "It exists outside the flow of time, where matters can get the attention they so deserve, unfettered by the nagging tug of clocks and calendars."

"Look, Fido," Ammit scolded. "We don't have time to give the grand tour to every life-challenged tot that drops in to stink up our chamber. I have it on good authority that there's going to be a terrible roller-coaster accident very soon, so we've got to stay on schedule."

Milton crinkled his brow. "I thought this place didn't run on schedules?"

Ammit grimaced. "Even so, patience is a virtue, and there ain't any of that down here."

Ammit's stomach flopped and created waves of rippled gelatin. "Look, you're giving me an ulcer. Step down and have your eternal soul appraised before I bust a giblet."

Milton and Annubis arrived before the bronze scales. Milton looked around at the thousands of jars lining the walls. The dark, blobby contents seethed like angry lava lamps and knocked against the glass.

"What are those?" Milton asked.

Annubis made a grand, sweeping gesture with his arm. "These are lost souls, their owners unknown."

Milton scanned the rows of bubbling jars. "How can a soul get . . . lost?"

Ammit sighed wearily. "The question is, how come more souls *don't* get lost? We run on volume down here. Everything's gotta move, move, move. And sometimes in the process, souls just slip away—especially the light ones—floating around looking for their bodies and causing all sorts of trouble. Those vicious, sooty gobs are especially nasty. Little piranhas, they are. So we keep 'em jarred up tight."

Milton fidgeted, shifting his slight weight from sneaker to sneaker. "How come they're all so black? Is that normal?"

The gelatinous demon smirked slyly. "Nice try, pipsqueak. You can't put off eternity. Stop stalling and let's start appraising. ANNUBIS!"

The dog god pressed his paw hand lightly against Milton's back. Milton quivered. "What are you going to—"

Annubis patted Milton softly. "Shhhh . . . it will only hurt more if your mind is busy and agitated. Relax. Concentrate on . . . *nothing.*"

Milton closed his eyes and, despite the thumping of his heart, tried to empty his thoughts. Annubis rubbed his hands together in tight circles until they radiated warmth. He closed his eyes, panted a bit, and then put one hand on Milton's head, and the other on his upper back. Slowly, Annubis's hot hands slipped into Milton's body. Milton groaned as electric warmth surged outward from Annubis's hands. It was deeply unsettling to have someone routing around inside you.

Annubis rummaged around Milton delicately, his fingers searching for something, like a surgeon hunting for a tumor. Then, the dog god let out a little yelp. "Got it," he murmured.

It was creepy, Milton thought. It was like having fingers wrap around all of your emotions, all of your memories . . . everything. Then, with a gentle tug, Annubis withdrew his hands, and Milton screamed.

In Annubis's smooth hands was a long, wriggling blob. It was like a stretched-out jellyfish, constantly shifting its inner goo. Unlike the blobs in the jars, this one was brightly colored, a shimmering rainbow of gorgeous gunk.

But to Milton the blob wasn't beautiful or ugly or anything at all, really. It was as if he had been submerged in a Grand Canyon filled with cold despair and infinite absence. He felt numb, lifeless, yet in unendurable agony. Everything about him that was "Milton" had been ripped away. In Milton's mind, it was the worst feeling, or nonfeeling, that anyone had ever felt—or not—*ever.*

Annubis delicately juggled the struggling blob between his two hands like a Slinky, until one hand held a rich clot of swirling colors and the other, a small speck of black. Carefully cradling the goo, he set the brightly colored mass on one tray of the scale and the dark pebble on the other.

Ammit secured Milton's restless, wiggling soul to the tray with a silky net.

"This one's got a lot of spirit," mumbled Ammit.

"Odd . . . There's barely anything weighing it down. I've never seen one like this here . . ."

Just then Ammit's headset chirped. "Hecko, you've reached the Assessment Chamber, this is Ammit speaking, how may I direct your call?"

"Nice of you to finally pick up," Bea "Elsa" Bubb squawked from the tiny receiver. "I called to see if a certain boy has shown up yet. His name is Milton Fauster. He's a scrawny nuisance who asks too many questions for his own bad."

Ammit raised a row of ingrown hairs above his eye that must have been eyebrows at some point. "Why, yes, Principal Bubb. He's right here."

"Excellent," she said. "There seems to be an . . . *inconsistency* . . . in his file. I'm sure it's nothing to be concerned about. After all, it's not like the Galactic Order Department has ever made a *mistake,* and it's *certainly* no error on our part . . . *ha ha ha* . . . So until this is all sorted out, we need him under our *thumb,* if you take my meaning."

Ammit smiled. "Yes, your vileness. Understood. You can count on me."

"I doubt that," Bea "Elsa" Bubb answered. "But just make sure you do my bidding and keep this little chat under your jelly, or else there'll be heck to pay. Have a nice day."

She hung up.

Ammit began adjusting the scales. The tray holding the colorful glob of liquid energy touched the smooth, alabaster table, while the dark speck was teetering in the air. He grimaced.

"Um, Annubis," Ammit said. "Is that a zombie squirrel in the corner?"

Annubis whipped his head around and sniffed the air hungrily. Ammit pressed his thumb on the scale until the tray holding the black speck touched the table while Milton stared blankly off into space, shivering.

"Wait," Annubis whimpered. "The chamber is round, there aren't any corners."

"Oh," Ammit responded while writing some figures down in his clipboard, "my mistake."

Ammit removed his swollen jelly thumb from the scale. Next he took a tiny silver spoon with serrated edges and gently scraped the side of Milton's soul, scooping up a small pea-sized glob. Ammit put the glistening bead into a plastic bag, wrote "Milton Fauster" on it with a grease pencil, then added it to dozens of others stacked in the creature's out basket.

"Anyway," he continued, "looks like we're done here. Go get the next bygone brat."

Annubis trotted back to the scales and examined the black speck. "But it's so small."

Ammit squirmed. "Yes, but it must be terribly dense," the creature said. "He must have committed one last doozy of an offense. That's enough to keep you down here."

The dog god sniffed Ammit, unconvinced. "Are you sure?"

"Of course I'm sure," the jelly-like demon countered. "Don't you trust me?" He gestured to his exposed internal organs. "It's not like I could hide anything from you."

Annubis shrugged his shoulders and sniffed the paralyzed Milton. "Fine, then. Let's give him his soul back, quickly. This is cruel."

"Okay, goody four-paws. Here you go."

Ammit handed Annubis back the boy's eternal soul.

Swiftly Annubis took the multicolored goo and gently placed it back inside Milton. Instantly the light blazed back into Milton's formerly dull eyes.

"You'll get your results from the Department of Unendurable Redundancy, Bureaucracy, and Redundancy," Ammit said hurriedly, "when they're good and ready. But from what I've seen, I wouldn't plan on leaving anytime soon."

As the creature jiggled with laughter, Milton turned to Annubis with desperation.

"I can't stay here," he said with panic. "It's all a big mistake."

Ammit rolled his eyes. "Get him out of here," he gurgled. "We're as clogged and backed up as Principal Bubb's toilet."

Annubis led Milton toward the door.

"There's got to be some way . . . ," he murmured.

"Come," Annubis said softly.

He helped Milton out of the chamber. As they walked through the doorway into a hall congested with confused, frightened boys—all of them looking convinced they were simply having one heck of a nightmare—Annubis leaned down near Milton's ear and whispered, "I can tell you don't belong. I can smell it. I'm a great judge of character. All I can suggest is that you get a copy of your contract and look for any . . . discrepancies."

"ANNUBIS!" yelled Ammit. "BAD DOG! Get in here with another boy right now or so help me I'll have you neutered."

Annubis yelped. He straightened up and achieved his former, imposing self. "Next!"

Milton scanned the hallway, looking lost. "What do I do now?"

Annubis grabbed the hand of a red-haired boy wearing Scooby-Doo pajamas. The boy giggled. "Big doggy!"

"Down the corridor to your right," Annubis barked. "For your fitting."

9 · OUT OF FASHiON

MILTON POKED HIS head into a vast tiled room where rows of boys shivered in their underwear. Immediately a small withered demon grabbed his hand and pulled him inside.

"Quick," it croaked.

For eternity, Milton thought, everyone sure seemed to be in a hurry.

"Give me your clothes," the demon prodded, "and that backpack."

Milton gulped. He could feel Lucky squirming, coiling, trying to get comfortable. Irritated, the demon dug its claws into the knapsack. Milton could just barely make out Lucky's telltale hiss.

"Wait," Milton blurted. "This knapsack is important to me. Full of memories of . . . *up there.*" He paused.

"On second thought, take it. Those memories would only torment me for all eternity."

"Hmmm," the demon considered. "Good point. Ha-HA! I command you to keep your sack of excruciating anguish!"

"Oh no," Milton said flatly. "You tricked me, you devious creature of pure unquenchable evil, you."

The demon sneered, thoroughly pleased with itself.

Milton breathed a sigh of relief. Outwitting a demon was easier than he had expected. He slipped off his navy blue corduroys and sensible, button-down L.L.Bean shirt. After taking his clothes and depositing them in a large Dumpster, the demon sporked Milton in the bottom, herding him with the other boys into a beige waiting room carpeted with filthy shag.

"What's going on?" Milton asked a skinny Asian boy next to him.

The boy looked at him with shock. "You're not real. This place isn't real. It's all a bad dream. I'm going to wake up any moment."

Milton nodded and smiled. "Yes, all a dream."

A bald, round man in a bright pink leisure suit strutted in pushing a wardrobe on wheels. On dozens of hangers hung the same horrible outfit: bright yellow lederhosen.

"Bonjour, mesdemoiselles," he said elegantly. "I am

Mr. Dior, and it eez my unfortunate duty to ensure that each and every one of you looks simply hideous."

Milton obediently buckled up his wool lederhosen, secured his plaid cap, tied his checkered kerchief, pulled up his lime green kneesocks, and slipped into his splintery wooden clogs.

The boys stared dumbfounded at each other. The definition of "dreadful" just kept expanding with every passing minute that didn't pass.

"*Sacré bleu,*" Mr. Dior deadpanned. "If ze looks could kill, you lot couldn't harm a chronically ill gnat."

The skinny Asian boy looked at Milton. "That's the last time I have triple-cheese pizza right before bed."

A bug-eyed demon with a great big camera scurried into the room.

Mr. Dior glided over to the wall and yanked down a paper backdrop from the ceiling. It was a mural of fire, brimstone, and nasty devils flogging tormented men and women. The boys were lined up against it.

"Hmm . . . ," murmured Mr. Dior. "Something's not quite *exacte.*"

He surveyed the line of grotesquely dressed children and settled on Milton. After a moment of scrutiny, he took off Milton's cap, spat a glob of phlegm in his palm, and rubbed it into Milton's hair until it stuck up in every direction.

"There," Mr. Dior said while screwing Milton's cap back on. "Simply *affreux.*"

Milton trembled, mortified. To say he had a thing about germs was like saying that Marlo had a thing about taking what wasn't hers. After washing his hands in a public restroom, for example, Milton would use a paper towel to turn on the hand dryer, then get another paper towel to open the door, and then get yet another paper towel to open the lid of the garbage to throw all of his accumulated paper towels away, which made him want to wash his hands again.

Now he had the loogie of some dead Frenchman dripping down his scalp.

"Smile," the bug-eyed demon ordered and, with an explosive pop of a flashbulb, the image of a dozen or so sniffling boys in scratchy yellow lederhosen was preserved for all eternity, or until they turned eighteen, whichever came first.

10 · YOU ARE
UTTERLY ALONE

"GET IN ZE line with ze first letter of your last name," Mr. Dior had told them. But in this new room of damp concrete and lost boys arranged in rows, Milton was, again, perplexed. The signs above the Disorientation Assignment counter read "A–F," "F–K," "K–P," "P–U," and "U–Z." Fauster, F . . . did that mean he was supposed to be in the first or second line? Lapses of logic like this were especially bothersome to Milton whose whole life was arranged *just so*. He decided to pick the first line, despite knowing deep down he would somehow be wrong.

"Wrong line," the decomposing man behind the counter confirmed when Milton finally got to the front.

"But my last name is Fauster . . . this line says 'A to F.'"

"Yeah," the grumpy man grumbled through purple, peeling lips, "But your last name isn't 'F,' is it?"

"No," Milton admitted, "but it's rather misleading . . ."

"Take it up with Principal Bubb, then. In the meantime, you'll have to stand in the other line. Here's something to read while you're waiting. Next!"

Milton reluctantly took the pamphlet the man pushed toward him. He got to the very back of the next line, prepared to do what you apparently did in Limbo: wait.

SO YOU'RE DEAD
A PAMPHLET FROM CHILDREN IN NETHERWORLD CONVERSION HELP (CINCH)

Dying is one of the most important parts of being alive—the *last* part! Your young mind is more than likely crawling with conflicting thoughts, emotions, and questions.

First, let's start with a little story . . .

BECKY AND VELMA:
A TALE OF TWO AFTERLIVES

This is Becky. She passed on after being in a coma for fifteen months. She doesn't know what to do. Poor Becky. She looks like she's freaking out!

This is Velma. She arrived here after touching a poisonous frog on a camping trip. She is dealing with her new circumstances calmly and with an open mind. Doesn't she look at home in the hereafter?

Becky is depressing everyone with her constant crying and negative attitude.

Velma, on the other hand, is making lots of new friends. How does she do it? Velma doesn't make any trouble and trusts that the Powers That Be have her best interests in mind. She makes the most of her untimely death. After all, when the afterlife serves you lemons, make lemonade!

Becky upsets everyone by asking too many questions. Why can't she just respect authority? Maybe she'd have more friends if she smiled more!

Look: Velma has been elected student decomposing body president! This girl is going straight to the top!

Uh-oh. Looks like Becky has to clean the girls' bathroom with her toothbrush for talking back to her den demon. The only place this girl is going is straight down. I hope she likes it hot!

Be like Velma and passively accept your afterlife. Why make waves when you can make a splash!? So what's the moral of this story? Don't be like Becky!

THE TRANSITION FROM THE REAL WORLD TO THE BEYOND IS A MAJOR CHANGE. HERE ARE SOME TIPS FOR A SMOOTH MOVE:

• Just because you're dead doesn't mean you can be lazy. Sure, you may be six feet underground, but that doesn't mean you can't hit the ground running!

• Once you get settled you'll start thinking about making new friends. Don't expect them to be knocking on your crypt to meet you. Go out, mix it up, and start engaging with interesting spirits. Here are some conversation starters to get you going: "Hi! Who were you?" "Wow, you look great! Did you die in your sleep?" "Is it cold/hot here, or is it just me?"

• As much as you'd like to stay in touch with old family and friends, it's just not possible. They're going on with their lives, and you're not. That's just how things go.

GOT QUESTIONS?
WELL, WE'VE GOT ANSWERS!

Why do I have to keep going to school? Isn't it bad enough that I'm dead?

Wow, sounds like someone woke up on the wrong side of the coffin! Just because you cease to be doesn't mean you cease to learn. To prepare you for your adult afterlife, you'll be attending a variety of classes to help you become a well-rounded entity. Depending on your annual report cards, you could be going up, down, in between, maybe even reincarnated! Who knows? (Well, except the Galactic Order Department, that is!)

What do I do if I'm not happy in the afterlife?

Oh, boo-hoo. Looks like someone needs their diaper changed! If you are feeling homesick, get over it. Try joining a club or afterlife organization (like maybe the Whiny Kids Club). It's a great way to meet and interact with others who share similar interests.

This isn't what I expected at all!

Hey, that isn't even a proper question! Some recently deceased have expectations about the hereafter before arriving. Some look forward to it and are eager to experience their last adventure. Others may feel it falls short of their expectations. These feelings are typical. Experience them. But don't wallow. Remember when you were alive and everyone wondered what it was like on this side? Well, as a new resident, at least now you know the answer!

YOU ARE UTTERLY ALONE

Each young spirit experiences "the change" in a unique and individual way. Sure, it can bring feelings of fear, sadness, confusion, doubt, and a sense of loss. While these feelings are perfectly normal, they are still nothing to be proud of.

C'mon . . . snap out of it, Gloomy McSad! The passage from the land of the living to the land of the dead is an exciting one! With a positive outlook you might actually enjoy this new phase of your nonexistence.

Now, being dead isn't so bad after all, is it?™

"Next!" the blue-haired demoness behind the counter hissed. Startled, Milton dropped his pamphlet on the floor and shuffled to the counter.

"Um, y-yes," he stammered. "Fauster . . . I'm here to be, uh, disorientated."

The creature snorted and leafed through a stack of files, plucking out a slender folder. She stamped it with a loud thwack and pushed it across the counter.

"There you go . . . Next!"

Milton stared helplessly at his folder. "Is that it?"

The demoness glared at him, her yellow eyes flaring like coals. "What do you want? A parade? Fireworks? A big party? You're not the first kid here and you're definitely not the last."

"But what do I do?"

The impatient creature sighed. "I'll talk slowly so you can understand. *This is your class schedule and registration packet.* Your first class starts . . . *started* . . . five minutes ago. Tsk, tsk . . . looks like you really are the *late* Milton Fauster." She giggled like a hyena laughing at its struggling prey.

"How can I be late if there isn't any time here?" Milton asked.

The crusty blue-haired clerk scowled. "Be that as it may, it doesn't stop you from being tardy," she croaked impatiently. "Better hurry. Don't want to start off on the wrong hoof."

Milton clomped out of the room and into the hallway in his painful wooden clogs. The hall was flooded with wavering, headache-inducing fluorescent lights. Flaming torches also jutted from the walls, filling the halls with a sooty smoke that made Milton's eyes burn. All of Heck's passages, it seemed, were filled with an incessant and unsettling howling, apparently for no other reason than to be unnerving.

He knelt down and carefully removed Lucky from his knapsack. The ferret winced at the harsh light.

"Lucky," Milton whispered while scratching his wriggling pet's neck, "I need you to do something. Remember that bad lady's office? The one with the stinky, three-headed dog?"

The ferret looked into Milton's eyes, hissed, and shivered from his wet little nose to the tip of his tail.

"Good," Milton continued. "I need you to get my contract. It's in the file cabinet by her desk. It should be easy enough for you to find, because it will be the only one that smells like this . . ."

Milton bit his finger until it bled, then wiped it under Lucky's nose. The ferret's nostrils flared and a wild look came over him. He obsessively licked Milton's wound until the bleeding stopped.

"Okay, boy," Milton said sadly. "Time to go."

He gave Lucky one last squeeze, then sent him rippling down the hall like a fuzzy white wave.

Milton wiped away a tear, then opened his registration folder.

"Ethics, Room 1972," he muttered. "Teacher: Mr. R. Nixon." He stared down the hall. "No way, it couldn't be."

11 · CLASS CUTUP

MARLO SLICED CAREFULLY through the demon's tough skin—dark, crinkled rawhide mottled with red splotches—until she had made a deep, Y-shaped incision from shoulder to shoulder.

"Bonny good, Miss Fauster," said Ms. Mallon, the stout demon teacher of Marlo's demon biology class. "Yer a natural, ya are."

Marlo seemed to be the only student remotely interested in today's topic. In fact, the other girls—who were all wearing drab burlap muumuus, stirrup pants, and Birkenstocks with white socks—grimaced with disgust. Perhaps it had something to do with the fact that the demon body Marlo was currently dissecting belonged to her still-conscious teacher.

"Ooooh," Ms. Mallon shivered. "Watch it, luv.

Those instruments are colder than a Brit's Christmas in Belfast, they are! Ouch . . . a little deep, dearie."

"Sorry, Ms. Mallon," Marlo said while folding back a flap of cold, black skin from her teacher's chest. The whole experience was like peeling a really, really ripe banana that talked.

"Please, dear, call me Mary . . . *Typhoid* Mary," the plain, thick-featured teacher said in her coarse yet lilting brogue.

"Typhoid?" said Lyon Sheraton, a thin blonde with bulging blue eyes. "Isn't that, like, some old hippie band that does that song about money?"

"You mean Pink Floyd," said a sullen, freckled girl in the back of the class. "My mom worked in a hospital. She said that typhoid was a form of salmonella or something."

Lyon stared blankly at the girl.

"What happens if I connect the dots on your face? Does it spell *loser*?" she spat out like a verbal slap. Lyon smirked to her friend, Bordeaux Radisson, who—with her gleaming blond hair, vacant blue eyes, and frightening lack of body fat—seemed almost like a fashion accessory of Lyon's that she kept close to both accentuate and confirm her own hollow beauty.

"Salmonella," Marlo said. "Sounds like a fairy tale about a fish."

Lyon and Bordeaux shot Marlo a frosty stare, before Lyon broke it off with a dismissive eye roll.

"Quiet, lasses, before I have ya all quarantined," Ms. Mallon said. She sat up suddenly, causing some of the more squeamish girls to squeal, and brushed back her matted auburn hair.

"Thank ya, Miss Fauster. That'll be quite sufficient."

Marlo stepped away from the breached demoness as she carefully tugged apart the flaps of spotty skin, exposing her dry, lifeless internal organs. Lyon gasped.

"That is, like, so gross! If my stomach wasn't stapled, I'd barf all over the place!"

Ms. Mallon glared at her with dark, glassy slits. "Remind me to judge yer insides when they're hangin' out of *you* . . . which might not be too long with your attitude."

Lyon rolled her eyes and scowled.

"Scoot yer desks closer, you miserable young maidens," Ms. Mallon commanded. "And, Miss Sheraton, please refrain from vomitin' inside of me chest cavity."

The teacher straightened up and pushed her gaping chest out.

"Now, lasses, do any of ya know how a demon becomes a demon?"

The girls looked at one another blankly. Marlo shrugged her shoulders as she stood beside her cleft teacher. A pudgy, cruel-looking girl with hairy knuckles answered. "Doing something really, really bad?"

"Well, that's a given," Ms. Mallon replied. "Here, let me show you something."

Ms. Mallon carefully spread the opening in her chest wider, producing a few pops and tears. She reached her claws deep into her chest cavity, pried apart her withered lungs, shifted her prunelike heart, and revealed something so startling that even Marlo stifled a squeal. Inside Ms. Mallon was . . . a miniature Ms. Mallon. Not a wrinkled, demon shell . . . but a plain, plump human, with reddish-brown hair, ruddy cheeks, and a thin-lipped smirk. The miniature Ms. Mallon was like an extra internal organ, living just behind the withered heart, mostly just a head with a wasted, freakishly small body. All Marlo could do was chuckle. Her teacher was a huge, terrible candy bar with a living, nougatty center.

"That is, like, *so wrong*," commented Bordeaux.

"I assure you, broomstick, 'sno more wrong than havin' liposuction on yer twelfth birthday," the demon teacher replied. "What happens is, once yer down here long enough, yer body 'forgets.' Its mem'ry, which is all it really *is* at this point, fades away, slowly like, becomin' less distinct, as if it were lost in a Londonderry fog. And so it begins to lose its struggle."

"What do you mean by 'struggle'?" Marlo asked.

"The struggle between our inner and outer identities, luv," Ms. Mallon replied. "The tension between who we are inside, and who we are on the outside. A demon isn't some random, bloomin' monster dreamed up by the Big Guy Downstairs. We're simply people—

granted, wicked *diabhals* sent to *ifreann*—turned inside out."

Lyon's collagen-fattened lips gaped like a bigmouth bass out of water. "You're telling me that, like . . . you were a person?"

Ms. Mallon—both outwardly and inwardly—sneered. "Yes, wretched child. I was not unlike you, so very long ago."

Bordeaux snorted. "I *so* don't think so."

"Well, I may 'a been a touch more . . . full-bodied than you—yer thinner than a French fry in a potato famine—but I had quite an infectious personality."

Bordeaux absentmindedly scratched several small red blotches that had just appeared on her lower neck.

"You can only conceal what's in ya fer so long before all that was in is hangin' out," Ms. Mallon said.

Lyon shook her carefully maintained mop of blond hair. "You sound like a bad fortune cookie. Look, I'm sorry you're, like, a big, dried-up piece of rotten meat or whatever with a lady stuck inside, but whatever happened to you isn't going to happen to me." She sucked in her cheeks and put her bony hands on her nonexistent hips. "Besides, my daddy will get me out of here. He's, like, *so* rich. He probably owns this place."

The teacher laughed, which made her useless internal organs jiggle disturbingly, then sat up stiffly.

"Miss Fauster, would ya do me the honor of stitchin'

me back up? This is most uncomfortable, and yer the only one present I would trust with such a procedure."

Marlo looked around uncomfortably. "Um . . . sure."

As Marlo stepped up and took the needle from Ms. Mallon, she heard Lyon whisper to the rest of the girls. "Ooh, looks like Elvira is teacher's gross new pet."

There's something about a girl's whisper that manages to slice through the air like a knife, arriving louder and sharper than a scream. Marlo had never, ever been considered anything remotely petlike in relation to teachers. Not even a tolerated stray. It was a new feeling, and she didn't like it. She felt like taffy pulled in two directions.

On the one hand, she wanted to fit in with the other bad girls. She could never *really* fit in anywhere, but she was much more comfortable in the role of class pit bull than lapdog. On the other hand, Ms. Mallon was kind of cool, or as cool as a fat, contagious demon could be. The class was actually kind of interesting. Still, even an outcast as, um, *outcasty* as Marlo was not immune to the slings and arrows of peer pressure. She needed to regain her balance in the scheme of things, or perish yet again.

"So," Marlo said while suturing her teacher closed, "can you explain that 'tension' thing you were talking about?"

Bordeaux and Lyon leaned into each other, snickering.

"Good question," Ms. Mallon answered. "It's the tension of identity. The eternal war between appearance and substance. Sooner or later, our true selves prevail."

"Mmm-hmm," Marlo mumbled as she snuck her skilled, pickpocket's fingers into her teacher's abdomen. She clutched on to something in the middle of her teacher's chest. Deftly, she plucked what was surely Ms. Mallon's heart from its supposedly final resting place. It was like yanking a large, overripe grape from a vine. Marlo slyly displayed the stolen organ at her side, blocked from her teacher's sight by a steel tray, so that the other girls could see how gifted she was. But instead of a chorus of giggling appreciation for her "inside job," all she heard was a muffled squeal ratting her out.

"Our heart!" a shrill voice exclaimed from her teacher's chest cavity. "The little nasty stole our heart!"

Ms. Mallon snapped out of her philosophical musing at the shouting from within her chest. Marlo's pale face reddened while the girls finally giggled, but at Marlo's expense.

"Miss Fauster," the teacher said softly, "though it has grown cold and hard, I would appreciate it immensely if you would return my heart to its rightful place. It may not be much, but it has great sentimental value."

Humiliated, Marlo reopened Ms. Mallon's incision

and resecured her heart to the network of dried branches in her chest. The pinched face inside stuck its tongue out at Marlo.

"Thanks a lot, you little snitch," Marlo replied under her breath.

"Now, dear," Ms. Mallon scolded. "We all have a wee voice inside that's hard to silence, don't we?"

It was weird, thought Marlo as she stitched Ms. Mallon up yet again. She had once had a voice inside, when she was a little girl, but after years of ignoring it, it had finally grown quiet. She had thought she heard it whisper when she had taken her teacher's heart, but its warning had seemed as faint as a soft, cautioning breeze. She didn't like it. Things were bad enough without a nagging little voice making trouble inside, too.

Just as she was nearly finished sewing up her teacher, her needle hit something hard. A bone. She slipped her thumb and index finger subtly inside the wound. It felt like a rib. It must have been dislodged during her failed attempt at stealing her teacher's heart. The word "failed" blinked like lurid neon in Marlo's mind. Swiftly, she pulled the rib through the slit and up into her sleeve. *Perfect,* Marlo thought. *No witnesses.*

A faint voice bubbled up from inside Ms. Mallon.

"Ya thievin' magpie!"

Quickly, Marlo stitched closed the incision.

"Thank you, Miss Fauster," Ms. Mallon said while

clutching her chest. "Ooh," she winced. "Must be me heartburn actin' up again. Anyway, class. What was Miss Fauster here exhibitin' that is important to note?"

The girls all turned to Lyon, who had seemed to become their de facto leader. All the jockeying for power that boys did so loudly and obviously, girls could establish almost invisibly.

"A colossal lack of judgment . . . and style," Lyon responded tartly.

The girls tittered maliciously. Marlo blushed, which is extra embarrassing for a Goth girl.

"Actually," Ms. Mallon said while buttoning up her red leather blouse, "Miss Fauster was unwittingly carryin' out one of the most essential aspects of biology, or how it's practiced down here, anyway. That would be a . . ."

The teacher scanned her pupils' faces for the smallest spark of understanding, but there wasn't a glimmer. She sighed.

". . . *forensic examination:* the revealin' of circumstances and the securin' of evidence. In the afterlife, we couldn't give a right darn about how life is made. What concerns us is how it was *un*made.

"Once the exact conditions of death are assessed, one can trace the path that the spirit will most probably follow. This information is of extreme interest to both the Powers That Be and the Powers That Be Evil, especially when settlin' disputes. Without actual proof, an allegation is as worthless as a comb to a bald man. It's just an assumption with airs."

She walked up to Marlo. Despite herself, Marlo winced. Her teacher wrapped her thin, sinewy arm around Marlo's shoulder.

"You have a light touch, luv," Ms. Mallon added. "I can see yer really goin' places. You just might have a brilliant career down here."

Marlo cringed. Lyon and Bordeaux glared at her from across the room. If looks could kill, those twin blue-eyed stares would be on *America's Most Wanted*.

She had accidentally made a bad situation worse, she thought as she stealthily tucked Ms. Mallon's ill-gotten rib into her pocket. Marlo, too, had been turned inside out. Up above, she knew her place: in the back of the class, making trouble. Down here those same instincts made her teacher's pet, the outcast of the outcasts. As Ms. Mallon tightened her claws around Marlo's neck, sealing her fate in the eyes of the other girls, she did indeed feel every inch a teacher's pet, with an exceptionally tight collar.

12 · FiRST-CLASS FRiGHT

MILTON CREAKED OPEN the door and walked into the sudden hush of a classroom, interrupted. Yep, there was no mistaking it. Standing in front of the class was Richard Nixon, the deceased thirty-seventh president of the United States, who had resigned in disgrace in 1974 after a big scandal called Watergate where he had tried to cover up a secret government conspiracy. The stooped, drooping old man was lecturing about ethics, of all things.

"The term comes from the Greek word *ethos,* which in the plural means 'character,'" Mr. Nixon said, his sagging jowls flapping as he spoke before the twenty or so terminally bored boys.

Milton crept toward the nearest empty desk, but it was near impossible to be stealthy in wooden clogs and bright yellow lederhosen.

"Ethical actions may be approved of in that they are good, desirable, or right," the teacher continued, undeterred by a chorus of loud yawns, "or disapproved of because they are bad, undesirable, or wrong . . . like being late for class."

Milton sat down at an unoccupied desk in the back of the class.

"As I was saying," Mr. Nixon carried on, "ethics is the study of moral principles and philosophical quandaries. A traditional philosophic question is whether right and wrong are fundamental in the nature of things, making them absolute, or merely relative to present circumstances, fluctuating on the requirements of the moment."

Mr. Nixon's bloodshot eyes settled on the class list on his desk. "Mr. Fauster," he said in a low, cutting rumble. "Since you know so much about ethics that you feel your attendance is optional, give us an example of the latter."

Milton hated being singled out like this, not because he didn't know the answers—he almost always did—but because he had to act like he didn't know the answers in order not to seem like any more of a freak than he already was. But his teachers *knew* that he knew the answers and took great pains to drag them out of him. This made Milton seem like a know-it-all to his classmates, and a head case to his teachers. Either the teachers were completely oblivious to the nuances of Milton's situation or—on some deep malicious level—cruelly aware.

"Um," Milton finally managed. "Like lying. Sometimes you lie to save yourself and others. Like when you lied about the whole Watergate thing . . . you probably thought you were doing the right thing, but each lie and criminal act kept taking you further and further away from what was right, or what you believed was right. Then, before you knew it, it was a big mess and you were impeached."

"Resigned," Nixon seethed. "Fully pardoned."

A blond boy with a head injury slapped his hand on his desk. "That's it! I thought you looked familiar. You're that crook from the history books!"

"I was NOT a crook!" Nixon bellowed. He opened his bottom desk drawer and switched off his tape recorder. "The decisions a president must make are very . . . *complicated*. And every situation, every time and place, has its own unique logic, its own ethical code, that no one outside could possibly understand. It's just like down here. Each circle of Heck is governed by its own principles, an all-encompassing logic, that hold it together."

Milton straightened up from his usual "don't notice me" slump and shifted to the edge of his seat.

"Within that logic is its own set of rules, a contract of right and wrong. If something—anything—maintaining that contract is proved unethical, the whole thing crumbles . . . like an administration built on lies . . . but that's all water under the gate, um . . . *bridge.*"

Milton scribbled notes on the back of his registration folder as the bell rang.

Mr. Nixon mumbled as the boys filed out of his class. "No respect for authority," he said while rubbing his gray, doughy face with his hands.

Contract . . . rings . . . own logic . . . rules . . . unethical.

Milton folded up his paper and stuffed it into his pocket as he fled the class. He hoped his faithful ferret was close to finding a way out of this awful place.

13 · SCENT UP THE RIVER

THE WORLD WAS a lot different when you were low. It seemed longer, higher, dirtier. Ferrets, it is generally known, have relatively poor eyesight. They do, however, more than make up for this weakness with their keen senses of smell and hearing.

Unfortunately for Lucky, the halls of Heck were knotted with sharp, distracting smells and strange, echoing noises that didn't seem to come from any one particular direction. The booming sounds never quite disappeared, either; they layered on top of each other until they formed a deep, unsettling roar.

One smell in particular sliced through the blend of pungent ammonia and decay: the biting musk of a particular three-headed heckhound.

Lucky followed the dark, twisting fumes until they became a taste in the back of his mouth. They led him to a towering ebony door carved with nightmarish monsters and, strangely, puppies and unicorns. The door was locked tight, though to a creature such as Lucky it posed no real obstacle. There was a small gap beneath the door, probably no more than an inch and a half high. Lucky possessed the rare ability to make himself almost completely flat. It was quite handy sometimes, like when Milton's aunt Agnes would visit and wrongly assume she could pet Lucky whenever she liked. It was harder to pet something stiff as an uncooperative board.

The twitching ferret slipped under the door and snaked across the floor of Bea "Elsa" Bubb's office, like a fuzzy white eel swimming in a shallow pond. He sniffed Cerberus's filthy velvet dog bed and nearly fainted. It was an assault to such a delicate instrument as Lucky's nose. Just beneath the stench was another smell, a familiar smell, a friendly smell.

The ferret skittered toward Principal Bubb's file cabinet that, lucky for Lucky, had been left slightly open.

Lucky slid inside and sniffed his way through the folders until he found the scent of his tall, hairless pet, Milton. At that moment, he heard the door creak open, followed by the heavy thump of hooves and the padding of paws. Lucky wasn't a creature of exceptional thought, but what he did think, he thought quickly. He grabbed Milton's contract with his sharp little teeth and began to chew . . . until he felt a pair of jaws—perhaps two pairs— seize his furry tail.

14 · SCIENCE FRICTION

THE AIR SEEMED dead, Milton thought as he watched his teacher prepare today's experiment. Stale, like the hot breath of a car left in the parking lot on a summer's day. Maybe he didn't even need to breathe anymore, Milton mused as he tried to free his arm, wedged between his torso and the sharp metal arms of his uncomfortably small desk chair.

Suddenly the air was filled with a sharp, sweet tang. It was a gross, saccharine, sugary smell, like dozens of overly glazed doughnuts locked away in a tomb for a million years, then suddenly exhumed. Milton's ears popped as an explosive gurgle of foam shot out of a beaker on the teacher's desk.

The sickly, bearded teacher jumped back and scratched his head. "Hmm . . . perhaps I went a little nuts with the high-octane corn syrup."

He sat up and scraped his name on the blackboard with his fingernail. "My name is Dr. Pemberton," he stated in a strange, hollow voice, "and I am your chemistry teacher." Dr. Pemberton coughed and smirked.

"Let's start off our class with a little joke. What do you do with dead chemists?"

He searched the empty gray faces of his students.

"Barium!"

Dr. Pemberton grinned hopefully, but all he got were blank stares and stifled yawns.

"Get it? *Bury 'em.* And because barium chloride is used in chemistry as a reagent in the preparation of . . . Oh never mind."

The teacher shook his head in exasperation, then turned to his chalkboard. As Dr. Pemberton leaned over to grab a stick of chalk, the side of his lab smock widened, and Milton saw a large, gaping wound where the man's stomach should have been. Apparently Milton wasn't the only student to notice.

"What happened to your belly?" asked a boy with a bandaged hand who was not just big for his age but for *anyone's* age.

"Maybe you ate it," snorted a short, redheaded thug to Milton's left. The class dissolved into wicked chuckles as the large boy with the bandaged hand—*Hey, the kid who got his hand stuck in the Automat*, Milton thought—slid down in his seat.

"If you must know, not that it's any of your business, I died of overcarbonation," Dr. Pemberton said indignantly. "My stomach one day just . . . blew up. It was incredibly painful, as fatal wounds go, and I would appreciate it if we could get back to the business of learning."

Dr. Pemberton walked over to a table covered with vials, beakers, liquids, powders, and Bunsen burners.

Milton raised his hand. "Excuse me, Dr. Pemberton. Not to dwell, but . . . how exactly does one die from overcarbonation?"

The teacher pressed his palms against the table, glared at Milton, and sighed deeply, producing a whistling rasp that fluttered his lab smock. "Well, young man, it was an unexpected occupational hazard from my particular brand of chemistry: sodalogy, better known as soft-drink science. See, I was the father of mass-marketed, consumer-focused carbonation."

He rubbed the tight, dark coils of his woolly beard in reflection.

"I was obsessed with trying to outdo myself, to concoct breakthrough beverages, each more delicious than the last. Then, one morning after a prolonged illness, I emerged from my sickbed to perfect my fizzvescent masterwork, which unfortunately left me with a sunroof for a stomach."

The redheaded boy picked his nose and yawned

loudly. "So, Dr. Gutless, did you make anything that anyone could actually drink?" The boy's beefy twin brother sniggered behind him.

Dr. Pemberton jabbed his finger in the air. "Another unsolicited comment like that, and I'll give you lot a pop quiz!"

He sat down and mopped his brow with a rag plucked from his lab coat. "Well, right out of the gate, I created my first, historic formulation, one which I cannot name due to a trademark agreement so all-encompassing that it even applies to the afterlife. But for every successful beverage in your local supermarket, there are thousands of quiet failures."

The teacher stared wistfully at the table of frothing beakers. "They all seemed like good ideas at the time. Nurse Pepper and Ms. Pibb were two sodas I made just for women, to capitalize on the suffragist movement. Mountain Don't and Six Down were two others that went belly-up before they could even go down anyone's throat."

Milton furrowed his brows. "If your drink was so popular, why are you here? Every kid I know loves soda. They can't get enough . . . oh . . . I get it."

Dr. Pemberton scowled and examined his class list. "Hmm . . . Mr. Fauster, is it? Thank you *so* much for picking at the scab covering my ultimate wound."

The teacher rifled through his desk drawer, pulled

out a Tums, and swallowed it. The tablet soon clattered to the floor.

"Apparently," he continued, "four out of five dentists are on the Almighty's board of directors."

With a mournful sigh, Dr. Pemberton put his handkerchief up to his nose. He inhaled deeply and shook himself out of his funk.

"Now, if we can focus less on me and more on our subject . . ."

The teacher rose, collected an armful of bound textbooks, and ambled down the aisle, plopping the heavy books down in front of the dumbfounded boys.

"Class—and I use the term loosely—it's time to pick a partner and make some chemistry!"

Milton and the grossly overweight boy were the two left after everyone else picked everybody else. The boy leaned toward Milton and inhaled deeply. "You smell like a s'more."

The boy's pupils expanded as he eyed Milton hungrily. Milton suddenly felt as if he were a particularly enticing item on a dessert tray.

"Uh, my name's Milton."

The boy snapped out of his hunger-induced hallucination. "I'm Virgil. Virgil Farrow," he said, offering his bandaged hand in greeting. Milton shook it gently, while the boy's small, kind eyes winced in pain.

"Sorry," offered Milton.

"Don't worry about it. It's my own dumb fault. I know the only decent food in that Automat is just bait in a trap. But still, sometimes my tummy has a mind of its own."

Milton was at a loss for words. Virgil was the first person in Heck who was actually conversing with him, not just yelling at him—other than Marlo, that is. He thought of that freaky pamphlet he had been given, *So You're Dead,* and the suggested conversation starters he thought he'd never need.

Milton cleared his throat.

"Who were you?" he asked cheerfully. "You look great! Did you die in your sleep?"

Virgil smirked at Milton. "That's funny . . . that stupid pamphlet . . . like that thing could help anyone."

Milton looked down at his Bunsen burner. "Yeah. Stupid pamphlet."

Virgil flipped through his ancient chemistry book.

"What about this?" he asked.

His sausage of a finger pointed to an experiment involving root beer and sulfur dioxide that, when mixed just so, was supposed to produce a soft drink that caused burps of poisonous yellow fog.

"Sure." Milton shrugged. "Sounds cool."

Virgil rifled through the drawer, searching for the right chemicals.

"So, anyway, you asked me who I was . . . ," he relayed sadly while scooping crystals into a beaker. "Just a normal kid, I suppose, only . . . bigger. I lived in Dallas, Texas, where everything is bigger, anyway. My last day was my birthday."

"That should make it easier for people visiting your grave to figure out how old you were," Milton said.

"Yeah," Virgil said, smiling. "That's something, anyway. So I was at I Scream, You Scream, that ice cream place that humiliates you on your birthday."

"Yeah, I'm all too familiar with it," Milton said. He shuddered.

"I had the Noah's Dark Chocolate Fudge Flood," said Virgil.

"Wow," Milton said in hushed, reverent tones. "I've never met anyone who actually ordered that."

"It's supposedly the most chocolate you can get without a prescription," Virgil said. "I can still taste it. So there I was, making my way through the Mount Ararat of sweet frozen cream when I felt something funny at the back of my throat, and definitely not of the 'ha-ha' variety. I looked down at my spoon and saw just one plastic hippo. And, you know, 'Twofer by twofer they went into the ark to Noah,' or whatever, so where was the other hippo? That's when it hit me—I was choking on it. A total goner. The waitress tried to give me the Heimlich, but she couldn't get her hands around me."

Virgil shook his head. "That's all I remember. Next thing I know is, I'm here. It seems like only yesterday . . . probably because it was."

Virgil smiled and looked over at Milton. "What about you?"

Dr. Pemberton glared at the two boys. "Less talk, more science," he snapped.

Virgil shrugged his shapeless shoulders and began scooping candy-colored chemicals into test tubes.

"I'll tell you later," Milton whispered. "But, as you can probably guess, it involved burnt marshmallow."

"Sweets will kill ya," Virgil mumbled as he blended his bubbly mixture. "But what a way to go."

"Well," Dr. Pemberton said as he wove his way between the lab stations, "let's see what we have here."

He inspected the experiments with obvious disapproval, grumbling under his labored breath. "Terrible. This lot wouldn't even make the grade as generic cola."

Dr. Pemberton examined an especially volatile mixture prepared by the hostile redheaded twins.

"Hmm," the teacher murmured as the bubbling, lava-like liquid gurgled over the test tube's rim. "Whatever this is, it isn't cola. But it might have some rewarding attributes nonetheless. Every night, all the sewage from the Stage goes through the River Styx down to . . . *the other place.* It would be an excellent way to unclog it when the sewage is especially nasty."

Milton and Virgil's mixture was murky and thoroughly unappetizing, with tiny bubbles that fell to the bottom and detonated rather than floating to the surface and delicately popping. As the teacher drew close to Milton's station, Virgil shook the concoction until it was a neon green sinkhole of exploding foam.

Dr. Pemberton examined their work.

"Hmm," he muttered. "Bubbles floating down. Not good. That's what my last experiment did," he added, absentmindedly patting his nonexistent stomach. "Well, slug it down, son. It's the only way to be sure."

Milton's eyes widened. "There's no way I'm drinking that."

Dr. Pemberton frowned. "Show some guts, boy."

"That's exactly what I'm afraid of!" Milton cried out. "I prefer my stomach intact, thank you very much!"

The class was totally still, though the teacher was vibrating like a teakettle set to blow. But before he burst, Dr. Pemberton patted his stomach and leaned against the lab station.

"You're giving me the second-worst stomachache I've ever had," he moaned. "Since you're taking up so much of my valuable time here in class, it seems only fair to rob you of some of yours. Detention. You. After school."

As Dr. Pemberton hobbled away to examine the handiwork of his other students, Milton contemplated his very first detention.

The word itself, "detention," was almost thrilling. It carried with it a slight tingling charge from the third rail of the wrong side of the tracks.

Milton had never once been given detention. It was fitting, somehow, in this nonsensical place, that he should be reprimanded for exhibiting common sense. Of course, good would be punished down here. And now Milton could taste what it was like to be a delinquent. Besides, detention in Heck would be like a holiday. He could read, write, draw . . . whatever. It could be like an all-expense-paid vacation from himself.

After the bell tolled, Virgil and Milton spilled into the hallway with the other boys.

Virgil burped loudly. He wiped telltale bits of green foam from his lips.

Milton's jaw dropped open. "You actually drank that? Are you trying to get yourself killed . . . *again?*"

Virgil shrugged his shoulders. "That which does not kill me only makes me gassy."

After another deep gastric rumble, Virgil stopped short and patted his ample tummy. "Whoa, that one had attitude," he said. "Anyhow, tough break about detention. That bites."

"How bad can it be?" Milton replied. "Just sitting in a room for an hour, relaxing, away from Principal Bubb."

Just then the other boys in the hallway scattered like cockroaches when the kitchen light turns on. From down the hall strutted Damian, apparently exempt from classes. He wasn't dressed in the humiliating wool lederhosen and clogs that all the other boys had to wear. Damian was sporting a black tailored suit, gleaming leather shoes with tassels, and a starched white shirt with monogrammed cuff links. Pinned to his lapel was a red badge reading HONORARY AIDE AND DEFECT ENFORCEMENT SECT (HADES).

Damian swaggered to Dr. Pemberton, who was closing up his classroom, and handed him a coiled parchment.

"What's this?" the teacher asked as he unfurled the scroll. Damian smirked at Milton as Dr. Pemberton read the note.

"Hmm," he said, then wiped crystallized sugar off of his beard and thrust the note back into Damian's hands.

"Teachers' meeting . . . Oh, good, Mr. Fauster," he said, noticing Milton loitering in the hall. "I won't be able to, um, *detain* you today, I'm afraid. So we'll just have to—"

"As a member of HADES, sir, I'm more than qualified to oversee such disciplinary actions," Damian offered in a strange new tone—cool, composed, efficient, and infinitely more disturbing than his usual loutish growl.

Dr. Pemberton shuddered, then gave Damian a nod. "Good," he said. "Thank you, Mr. Ruffino. I'm sure Mr. Fauster here will pose no problem, though be prepared to be barraged by a salvo of tiresome questions."

Damian smiled at Milton . . . bared his teeth, more like, exposing a freshly capped gold canine.

"We'll be like two peas in a pod," he said, wrapping

his meaty arm around Milton's trembling shoulder. "It'll feel more like recess than detention, right, Milty?"

For you, thought Milton gravely. *For me, it'll be like a game of dodgeball, with me as the ball.*

Dr. Pemberton walked away. Damian released his grip on Milton and caught up with the teacher.

"Excuse me, Doctor, but I'd like to discuss some new ideas I have for keeping disorder around here, if I may . . ."

Milton and Virgil stared at the two of them as they walked down the hallway.

"That guy is bad news," Virgil muttered. "Like, 'war declared, disease outbreak, little girl trapped in a well, Raffi on tour' bad news."

Milton was silent. He felt a chill creep up his spine watching Damian ingratiate himself with Dr. Pemberton. This was a side of Damian that Milton had never seen before—shrewd, calculated, and subtle. He had become part of the establishment and, with that, had access to all sorts of powers ripe for abuse.

The stress of impending detention held Milton in its kung-fu grip. Milton's grip on reality—kung fu or otherwise—seemed gone for good.

15 · A LUCKY BREAK

LUCKY SPUN IN his small cage, whipping around so fast that he became a white blur of anxious, captive energy.

"When it settles down," Bea "Elsa" Bubb said to Cerberus as they squatted beside the cage, "we can begin."

After a moment, Lucky lay panting at the floor of his cage, unable to free himself from his ferret nature, which is typically asleep for eighteen hours a day. He gave one last, hostile glare at his captors before slipping into unconsciousness.

Principal Bubb sneered with satisfaction. She pulled out a small, curving tube from the inner pocket of her snakeskin muumuu and poked it through the bars of the cage.

She pressed one end gently against Lucky's lower back and the other to her thin, scaly lizard lips and sucked. Her yellow eyes rolled back into her head as a small coil of pink and blue electricity sizzled out of Lucky and into her tube. She grimaced as though chewing several pieces of extra-strength aspirin.

"Eww," she mumbled. "Ferrets sure are musky . . . even their spirit strands."

Lucky shuddered as if having a bad dream. Bea "Elsa" Bubb delicately withdrew the tube from the cage, careful not to drop the electric worm dangling at the end.

"Don't worry," she muttered to Lucky. "You won't go pop, weasel. There's plenty of spirit where that came from. You'll barely miss it."

She delicately placed the tube against Cerberus's trembling lower back.

"It's okay, my sweet, tri-headed prince," she cooed. "You won't like this, but we have to find the owner of this miserable, smuggled creature."

With the faintest of exhales, Principal Bubb sent the crackling coil of ferret energy into Cerberus. The hound from Heck gave a full-body quiver and, with a trio of small yaps, began to blister all over. Cerberus spun around with agitation. When he settled after a few moments, he was no longer who he was. He was, for all appearances, Lucky.

"Lucky" panted as Principal Bubb scritched the back of his neck.

"Settle down, dear. Your ghastly deformity is only temporary. Just one more thing and we can get on with this unfortunate charade."

She trotted back to her desk and opened her middle drawer, removing a small black velvet case. Inside was a pair of deep-red contact lenses. At the back of the drawer was a little white box with a screen, kind of like an old iPod with a few factory-unauthorized adjustments.

Principal Bubb squatted next to Cerberus. She held his newly ferretized head back and plopped the contact lenses in his eyes.

She patted his arched back. "There, there," she said.

She flicked on the box. On the screen was a grainy picture of herself as seen from Cerberus. The contact lenses warped her already warped face, creating a visual double negative that almost made a positive. *Almost*.

"Now, my love, my biddle tummy tum . . . I want you to root out our smuggler."

Cerberus twitched uncomfortably in Bea "Elsa" Bubb's arms.

"Yes, I know, that means mingling with those filthy guttersnipes, but no one said that upholding all that's wrong and vile would be easy."

She lovingly scooted Cerberus down the hall toward the classrooms. As the former dog bounded awkwardly away in its new body, Principal Bubb wiped away a speck of hard black crud that had oozed from her tear duct.

"Now be a pet, pet, and I promise that whatever you catch, you can keep."

16 · HATCHET JOB

IF TEDIUM WERE, say, a hurricane, Marlo thought in the back of class, then home ec would definitely be a Category Five.

Her teacher, Miss Borden, even looked dull: a round face with features that looked hastily sculpted in dough, a fussy hat pinned into mousy brown hair tied tight in a bun, and a dreary blouse buttoned up to her chin.

The only unbland things about her were her eyes—dark and dangerous as an abandoned well—and the fact that she was cutting out a dress pattern with an ax.

"Ladies," Miss Borden said with a voice like the crease in a freshly starched shirt, "to become a decent homemaker, you must look the part. And that means getting everything *just* right. Perfectly straight lines, and NO DANGLING THREADS!"

She chopped the gingham fabric with a mighty

whack. Marlo was dragged out of her daydream with a start. She wiped the spot of drool on her chin and pretended to be interested, or at least conscious.

"I apologize for the rude awakening, Miss Fauster," the teacher scolded. "But being a good seamstress takes precision and a pathological eye for detail. Likewise with other essential home economics skills such as interior design and cake decorating. How do you expect to make a tidy home if you don't pay attention?"

"I couldn't care less about making a 'tidy home,'" Marlo replied. "I already know how to sew, and I'm not interested in any of this happy-homemaker garbage."

The teacher glared at Marlo. "How do you expect to attract the attention of a potential husband? Certainly not with your charm and poise."

Lyon and Bordeaux traded wicked "Oohs" with each other. Marlo was beginning to feel like her old self: the source of class disruption. It felt good to be bad again.

"I'm not interested in a husband. He'd only slow me down. Besides, what kind of husband did all this bunk get *you,* anyway?"

Bordeaux whispered to Lyon, "I *knew* she didn't like boys!"

Miss Borden fumed. She seemed to be just a few snarky comments away from a meltdown. "I, to my eternal regret, never settled down with anyone other than my sister. I blame my parents. They were always . . . *in the way.*"

She stared at her ax with faraway eyes. With a shudder, she went from bubbling rage to arctic chill. This disturbed Marlo far more. Miss Borden left her sewing area and walked over to a basket in the far corner of the room.

"Well, future homemakers, in the event that you *do* one day meet Mr. Right, that will invariably lead to the ultimate fulfillment of every woman's great purpose: motherhood."

The teacher picked out a dozen small sacks of flour from the basket and swaddled each in either pink or blue blankets, before pinning the blankets tight with a safety pin so that the corner stuck out like a pointy little head. Next she put tiny pale pink or blue socks, depending, over the corners so that they looked like little fuzzy caps.

She stacked the lot in a wooden shopping cart and wheeled them down the aisle.

The girls gazed at one another with bewilderment. Bordeaux, however, clapped her hands and grinned.

"Dollies!"

Lyon elbowed her in the side as Miss Borden passed out the flour babies. The teacher handed Marlo a lumpy, gunnysack pouch wrapped in pink flannel. Lyon leaned into Bordeaux.

"Look, the vampire has a little baby bat," she jeered. "It's plain and shapeless like its mama."

Miss Borden turned sharply. "What is going on here, girls?"

Lyon turned coolly to address her teacher. "We can't concentrate with Marlo's constant grumbling."

"It's really distracting," added Bordeaux. "We're trying to learn how to become good homemakers, but—"

"Is there a problem, Miss Fauster?" the teacher asked tartly.

Marlo slunk back in her seat, plopping her doll on the desk. "No, ma'am. No problem."

"Good. Now, with your markers, give your darling bundles of joy a face. And be sure to name them. This will help you to establish a strong bond with your little one."

The girls, apart from the beaming Bordeaux, heaved a collective sigh and proceeded to scrawl features upon their flour babies.

"Don't forget the fangs, Vampira," whispered Lyon through pursed, candy pink lips.

Marlo seethed quietly as she drew a pony face on her doll. Whenever she was stressed, she found ponies strangely calming.

"And for those of you who think this is silly," Miss Borden announced, eyes trained on Marlo, "you've obviously never considered the financial advantages of babysitting."

The teacher took her ax and walked across the room toward the kitchenette.

"Now while you're getting acquainted with your

babies, I'll start preparing the ingredients for our class casserole."

She slid a stalk of celery across the counter, raised her ax above her head, and commenced chopping.

"One, two, three, four . . ."

Marlo tranced out, doodling on her flour baby, adding long eyelashes to its wet pony eyes. She couldn't stand this. She just had to score brownie points with the meanest girls she had ever met.

"Twelve, thirteen, fourteen, fifteen . . ."

Before she knew it, Marlo found herself leaning across the aisle to Lyon.

"Home 'Ick' with Miss *Boredom* more like, huh?"

Lyon gawked back at Marlo as if a park statue had suddenly come to life and addressed her. Marlo realized she hadn't earned so much as a brownie crumb.

"Twenty-seven, twenty-eight, twenty-nine, thirty . . ."

Lyon and Bordeaux exchanged looks. Then Lyon shot her perfectly manicured hand in the air.

"Miss Borden," she cooed in a skillfully sweet voice.

"Thirty-seven, thirty-eight, thirty-nine . . ." The teacher looked up as if awoken abruptly from a dream.

"Yes, Miss Sheraton. What is it?"

Lyon smoothed her shining blond hair demurely. "Well, teacher, I was trying to concentrate on caring for my new baby when Miss Fester interrupted me, calling you a boring old witch . . . that smells like dusty farts."

Lyon smiled innocently as the class held its collective breath.

Miss Borden's pupils dilated until her eyes were completely, unfathomably black. The full force of her glare was aimed straight at Marlo. What little color Marlo had in her face drained away. She swallowed hard, though her mouth was as dry as a cotton ball.

"I d-didn't," she stammered. "Well, not exactly."

Bordeaux murmured to Lyon behind her cupped hand. "Who's the baby now?"

Miss Borden whacked the ax into the table so hard that the oven door flung open.

"Forty!!"

Her rage again chilled suddenly, giving Marlo goose bumps. Miss Borden curled her thin, creased lips. "Miss Fauster," she said, overenunciating, "I'd like you to join me after school for a private tutoring session. I have an ax to grind with you."

17 · CAGEY CRITTER

LUCKY LICKED HIMSELF furiously while Bea "Elsa" Bubb squatted beside his cage, staring at him with revulsion.

"Disgusting creature," she grumbled. "As if something as repulsive as *you* could ever be cleansed."

She rose slowly, her dimpled knees popping in protest. "Well, the Galactic Order Department is always giving me grief about not serving fresh lunches," she snickered. "How would you like to join us for lunch, you fuzzy little entrée, you?"

Lucky stopped lapping to give Principal Bubb a long, heartfelt hiss.

"Oh, the feeling is more than mutual," she replied as she grabbed her lop-eared, dwarf-rabbit purse and headed out of her office. "We'll continue our little chat after my teachers' meeting."

The lizard lady chortled wickedly before slamming,

bolting, latching, and chaining the door behind her.

The incarcerated ferret gazed angrily at the door before continuing his personal hygiene regimen. He was determined to have the last lap.

Milton stared at his feet as he shuffled along the excessively lemony hallway, dreading his date with Damian. A familiar musk, however, poked through the chemical stench.

Milton looked up and saw a fuzzy, lumbering white blur billowing toward him.

"Lucky!" Milton squealed.

The ferret looked up suddenly, then ran into the wall at full speed. Milton rushed toward him and scooped the dazed creature into his arms.

"Lucky, you made it! Did you get my contract . . . ?"

Milton stared into his eyes. "Are you okay, little guy? Your eyes are kind of bloodshot . . . Hey, and where are your dice?"

The ferret blinked its wild, confused eyes and wriggled in what seemed like severe discomfort.

Milton wiped away goop from the animal's eyes and sighed deeply.

"It's okay, little guy," Milton whispered sadly. "It was a tall order, snatching a contract for a boy's immortal soul. I'm just glad you're all right."

Milton scratched the animal behind the ears—or

tried to, anyway—before it reared back and hissed. Milton gazed upon him with a look of parental worry.

"C'mon," he said, "let's get you something to eat. You don't seem like yourself."

As Bea "Elsa" Bubb clacked down a hall on her way to the teachers' lounge, her fuzzy bunny purse (with floppy ears and all) began to vibrate. She stopped, looked over her shoulder suspiciously, then fished her surveillance pod out of her bag.

She held the box in her scaly palm. Its tiny screen blinked red, casting her face in a lurid, scarlet hue. She jabbed the on button with her thumb, and a shower of static and snow danced on the screen.

"Hmmm," she mumbled. "Some kind of interference. As if he were in the presence of something, something . . ." Principal Bubb shuddered. *"Good."*

Through the geometric clouds of digital static emerged a gawky, concerned face dominated by a pair of broken glasses.

"I should have guessed," murmured Principal Bubb. "Milton Fauster, the rye seed in my dentures."

The screen went dark as the fake ferret was thrust, struggling, into the dim safety of Milton's backpack.

She smiled. "It's always good to have a mole, even when that mole is a demon dog in ferret's clothing."

18 · FLEE THiS CiRCUS

MILTON STRAIGHTENED HIS handwritten flyer, then pinned it to the bulletin board in the cafeterium.

MILTON'S PAIR OF DICE: LOST

"There," he whispered to the ferret tucked under his arm. "We'll find your collar. I'm sure that's why you're acting so weird."

He rubbed the panting animal's back, arriving at a cluster of swelling blisters by its tail. Milton frowned. "Why don't you take a nap in the knapsack while I get you some food? You don't look so hot."

The ferret flinched and squirmed as Milton stuffed him in the bag.

The cafeterium was full of nervous boys in search of something edible that, ideally, wouldn't maim them.

Aside from the baited Automat machines, the only other unusual thing in the cafeterium was a purple dinosaur with an idiotic grin humming inane songs. The needy creature lunged toward unwilling boys with the intent of hugging them.

On the old, broken-down television in the corner was the image of a freshly painted bench.

"As paint is exposed to air," droned the announcer, "it undergoes a painfully slow drying process. Here it is in real time . . ."

Several boys from Milton's chemistry class sat at a rusty metal table just beneath the TV. On top of it sat an unappetizing platter of overcooked broccoli and mushy cauliflower.

Milton walked over. Just before he arrived, the two beefy carrot-topped twins from class sidled up on either side of Milton's lab partner, Virgil, like two menacing bookends.

"Eat up, piggy," taunted the larger bully as he reached across the table for a fistful of tofu and shoved it into Virgil's face.

"Yeah," snorted the shorter redheaded thug. *"Sooie! Sooie!"*

Hunger and fatigue had stripped Milton of his usual caution.

"Hey, guys, leave him alone," Milton said, hovering just behind Virgil, who was slumped over his plate.

"Isn't this place bad enough without us turning against each other?"

One of the twins rose and answered Milton's question with an abrupt, two-handed shove. "Shut your pie hole, four eyes!"

Virgil muttered to himself. "Mmmm. *Pie.*"

"Better four eyes than no brain!" Milton countered defiantly, though his trembling lip gave him away.

The red-haired hooligan pulled back his fist like a cobra coiling to strike. "You scrawny little . . ."

But before the bully's fist could make a connection with Milton's face, an even larger hand wrapped around it in mid-punch.

"Now, now, there will be none of that," said the hand's owner, Damian, in his new, smooth-as-snakeskin manner.

The two apprentice bullies seemed to evaporate in Damian's presence, as if they had suddenly been demoted to the lesser of two evils.

Milton looked up into Damian's dark, inscrutable eyes suspiciously.

"Uh . . . thanks, I guess."

Damian grinned. His gold tooth glinted for an instant, like a spark in a dynamite factory.

"Don't thank me, old friend," he said with a queasy warmth. "I'm a pain artist, and like most artists, I prefer to work with a blank canvas. And I have a whole palette of painful new techniques I can't wait to experiment with during our little playdate later."

Milton's spine froze like a poisoned Popsicle.

Damian wrapped his arms around his apprentice bullies, and looked down upon them with a condescending affection.

"All right, all right . . . I guess just *one* little bruise won't spoil my next masterwork. But just one punch . . ."

Damian leaned toward Milton and removed his glasses.

". . . and keep it clean."

One of the redheaded tormentors snickered and, without hesitation, gave Milton a quick jab to the eye.

"Oww!" he yelped, clutching his burning eye.

Damian delicately put Milton's glasses back on, then grabbed the twin thugs by the scruffs of their thick necks and threw them toward the purple dinosaur.

"Noooooooooooo!" they cried in unison as the overgrown lizard scooped up the twins into his smothering Jurassic arms.

"I love you, you love me. Darned for all eternity . . ."

The happy creature suffocated the two struggling delinquents with kisses and dragged them away.

Damian straightened his thin black tie.

"I'll see beating you later . . . I mean, *be seeing* you later."

Damian strutted away, pushing several boys aside for no reason.

Virgil wiped his brow. "Thanks, man."

"Don't mention it," Milton mumbled painfully. "Really, don't. At least not until the swelling goes down."

He walked over to the Automat machines and searched for a particular slot. Milton stooped down, slid open the little glass door, and pulled out a sickening yet strangely comforting slab of liver. Beneath the glistening, soft pink gland, was a note. Milton looked around cautiously and snatched it up.

Milton,

As you can tell by the barely legible handwriting, it's me, your sister. I had a hunch you'd be needing another piece of liver. It's the girl's lunch, dinner, whatever period and I needed to let you know something: I'm going to escape. Really soon. I'm not sure how exactly, but you'll know when I try. Everyone will know probably. I know I haven't been the best sister, but, deep down, I think you're really not all that bad, for a little brother, anyway. If you need to get a hold of me before I bolt, let us correspond via liver since no one in their right mind would eat the stuff.

Later,

M

Milton stood motionless for a moment before thrusting the note deep into his lederhosen. He walked back to Virgil in a daze, grappling with new thoughts and emotions. Marlo was planning another escape. If she was successful, he would be left here alone. If not, what would happen to her? Most disturbing of all, though, was the glimmer of fondness that peeked out of the note. This meant that she was scared, and she was never scared, which was scary, especially to someone who always was. Scared, that is.

Virgil hovered closer. *He must be a close talker,* Milton thought. Milton's personal space, however, was more like a city block.

Then, as if he were about to burst from the pressure of a grand, wonderful, wriggling secret, Virgil said in a whisper, "I'm breaking out."

Milton removed his liver eye patch, put his glasses back on, and scrutinized Virgil's face. He had a dark mass of freckles between his upturned nose and gentle eyes. "Maybe it's your diet."

Virgil shook his head. "No, out of *here.* Tonight."

Milton leaned close to Virgil. "Really? How?"

Virgil patted the pocket of his bulging lederhosen. "I got a map. We'd be home by morning. So," he continued with an infectious twinkle in his eyes, "you with me?"

This was an excellent example of synchronicity, Milton mused: a coincidence that really *isn't.* But Milton had no idea how or when Marlo was planning to break out.

"Wait a second," said Milton, regaining his usual sense of caution. "How did you get a map?"

"I saw a guard get chewed out by his supervisor this morning for smiling, so I limped by, flinching and crying, begging the guard not to beat me again, because I can't help how loud I breathe. The guard got a promotion on the spot because I was so pathetic. Then, later, when I got out of the nurse's office because of my hand, the guard snuck up to me and dropped a rolled-up piece of paper at my feet. By the time I picked it up, he was gone."

"And you trust a demon guard," Milton said skeptically.

"I'm a trusting person," Virgil replied. "They can't take *that* away from me."

"I don't know," Milton mumbled. "It just seems too easy."

Milton watched the singing purple dinosaur corral a herd of unsuspecting boys for a group hug. Their screams made him tremble.

He sighed. *What did escape even mean?* Did he think it could be as simple as returning to his old life, already in progress, like waking up from a bad dream? Or would he be a ghost doomed to haunt some creepy mansion on the edge of town forever and ever, with only stray cats and kooks to keep him company?

Milton's thoughts were dragged back to his impending detention with Damian.

Not only had Damian somehow become more calculated and *fluent* with his cruelty, he had been given a blank check by the Powers That Be Evil to become as sadistic as he possibly could, for as long as he possibly wanted. And he was about to cash that check all over Milton. *Who knows?* Milton thought. Maybe Virgil's map would lead them out of this nightmare.

"Well, when you've lost your life, what else do you have to lose?" Milton said. Whatever escape meant, he decided, it couldn't possibly be worse than eternal darnation with Damian.

He sighed, wiped away a sooty smudge from his broken glasses, and grinned. "Let's get the *heck* out of here!"

MIDDLEWORD

To live in Limbo is to live in a pit full of not-so-quick-sand, waiting. Just . . . waiting. It's suffering without the torment.

What's the point of Limbo, you may ask impatiently, hoping to jump to a hasty conclusion? Well, just hold your skittish ponies, now. Limbo isn't just nothing. It's the excruciating awareness of nothing.

Think of Limbo as a big, slow spiritual laundry that is trying to cleanse you of impatience. Time doesn't pass, but that doesn't mean nothing happens: it just never happens fast enough. And in the waiting is the lesson.

You know when you're in the dentist's office, flipping through those horrible, ancient magazines like Livestock Today, Macramé World, Slug Fancy, and Modern Tax Adviser, *listening to music so* boring that it's barely music? And it's not only deadly dull, but the whole time that you're there doing nothing you hear the whine of the dentist's drill, the sound of someone trying to talk but they can't because they have a rubber glove in their mouth, and the thousand-year-old receptionist blathering on to her aunt Edna on the phone about the meat loaf she ate last night and how moist it was—ugh, the worst word in the English language, moist—and, to top it off, there's some toddler with sniffles in the corner banging the back of his chair against the wall.

This is Limbo. It's frustrating, irritating, and nothing happens fast enough because nothing is happening. It's like racing toward a horizon that you can never reach. It's like trying to catch a rainbow. It's like trying to empty the ocean with a spatula.

Limbo is a lot like growing up.

19 · THICKER THAN WATER

MARLO STAGGERED DOWN the hall, a look of almost animal desperation in her eyes. As she passed the sizzling torches on the beige concrete walls, she noticed a small glass box just outside of the girls' bathroom. Inside was a lever with the words PULL IN CASE OF WATER painted on it in bright blue letters.

Marlo bit her thumb and cased out the empty hallway. Convinced she was alone, she rubbed her huge silver skull ring, closed her eyes, then smashed it into the glass. Quickly, she thrust her hand into the box and pulled the lever. The instant she gave it a tug, the fluorescent lights shut off and flames belched from the ceilings.

Miss Borden came rushing out of her classroom.

"Water! Water!" the teacher screamed. "Everybody run! Water! This isn't a drill!"

Panicked, girls began to stream out of the classrooms and into the blazing hallway.

Meanwhile, Milton and Virgil walked out of the cafeterium just as plumes of flame began to shoot from the ceiling.

"What's going on?" Milton gasped.

"I don't know," Virgil replied, "but this could be our chance. Quick, let's go to the little boys' room. I have an idea."

Just then they heard a pair of hooves clatter down the hall. Virgil and Milton traded looks of sheer terror.

"C'mon." Virgil grabbed his friend by the sleeve. "We've got to skedaddle." The two boys and one fake ferret dashed down the crowded hallway that had now become a fiery, frenetic free-for-all.

Milton stared at the toilet. Actually, the word "toilet" was far too poetic a word for the dark hole that assaulted Milton's senses. Try "horrid, reeking pit." While the toilet in the boys' bathroom would have made even a sewer rat wrinkle its nose, to Milton the sight was far more traumatic, causing a full-body paralysis of pure revulsion.

Milton had acquired, during the course of his short life, the ability to hold his bodily fluids in check until safe in the clean sanctuary of his own bathroom.

It had been years since he'd seen the inside of a school restroom.

And Virgil wanted him to climb inside the stinking hole before him.

"It's the only way, man," Virgil explained. "Do you think I want to dive down into *that* either?"

Milton stared into the darkness, somehow transported thousands of miles away by his thoughts.

"It's always darkest before the dawn," soothed Virgil as he put his pudgy hand on Milton's trembling shoulder. "No guts, no glory. It's time to poop or get off the pot."

"I don't know what's worse," Milton mumbled, "that toilet or your clichés."

Virgil smirked. "I'll be right back. I know where I can score us a couple of teeny flashlights. I saw some this morning in the nurse's office when she/it/whatever fixed my hand."

Virgil left Milton to stew in his thoughts. He closed his eyes. His therapist had told him to go to his "happy place" whenever Milton was faced with an anxious situation, which was almost hourly. Milton's happy place was a musty library full of books. All he needed to do was pretend that the powerful stench that prickled his nose was the intoxicating perfume of paper, dust, and old wooden desks. This was simply a case of mind over fecal matter. And the only thing Milton had to fear was fear itself (*Oh no*, Milton thought, *Virgil's got* me *doing it now* . . .). Wasn't the remote possibility of freedom—not to mention the rightful possession of his eternal soul—worth tromping through a little poop? He had to, at the very least, give it a try. After all, how bad could it really be?

20 · TUNNEL OF DUNG

IT WAS BAD. Worse than bad. Terrible.

Filthy drops dripped. Filthy drips dropped. Terrible plops and splashes echoed through the dark, cramped pipeline. The smell was like a mixture of vinegar, socks, rotten milk, and every imaginable shade of poo. The smell was so thick, it was like a putrid blanket wrapped over . . . *everything.* And that was the opinion of just one of Milton's senses. The other four weren't wild about their present situation, either.

Two weak flashlight beams slashed through the hot, stinky blackness. Milton and Virgil crawled on all fours with the flashlights duct-taped to their heads. Milton panted, his nose curling, feeling as if his lousy liver lunch were trying to make a break for it.

"It stinks in here," he said in a colossal display of understatement.

"It's the . . . River Styx that . . . stinks," wheezed Virgil. "It's the sewage."

"So this is where it all goes?"

"Comes," Virgil replied while wiping grime off his face. "Remember what Dr. Pemberton said: all the sewage in the world comes through here, down to . . . *the other place.*"

Milton gagged as blobs of toxic crud slithered down the great pipe.

"It's like a disease buffet down here. What I wouldn't give for an industrial-sized drum of antibacterial soap."

Milton pulled up his shirt so it covered his mouth and nose. He looked like a germ-phobic bandit.

"So what's the plan?" he said, his voice muffled through his shirt.

Virgil pulled an ancient scroll from his knapsack and unrolled it. One side of the yellowing map featured a complex network of lines, curving and coiling like a convention of Krazy Straws.

"It says that if we follow this pipe here," Virgil said, highlighting a tract of plumbing with a smudgy finger swipe, "it should lead us to . . . the Secret Toilet, just outside the gates."

Milton's eyes peered out from above the collar of the shirt cinched tightly over his nose. *"The Secret Toilet,"* Milton repeated with disbelief.

"Yeah," Virgil replied with a hopeful twinkle in his eye. "Just outside the—"

"I heard you," Milton interrupted. "It's just so . . . *ridiculous*. Why on earth would—"

"We're not *on* earth, in case you hadn't noticed," Virgil said, interrupting Milton's interruption. "A secret toilet isn't any more bizarre than the other things we've seen down here."

Milton sighed. "I suppose," he conceded. "Can I see that map of yours?"

Virgil shrugged and handed his friend the map. Milton flipped it over and pressed his broken glasses up the bridge of his nose. The other side of the ancient map featured nine concentric circles: the Nine Circles of Heck. Virgil knelt next to Milton and jabbed his swollen finger at the center of the map.

"Here's Limbo. That's where we were."

He slid his finger down to a thick green ring on the map.

"Next is Rapacia, for greedy kids," Virgil said.

"Sounds like my sister," replied Milton somberly. "Speaking of my sister—"

"The Third Circle," interrupted Virgil as he studied the map gravely, "is Blimpo for . . . *plump* kids. I'm pretty sure that's where I'll end up."

Virgil pointed to a sketchy-looking ring that subtly seemed to shift every so often.

"Then there's Fibble for lying kids . . ."

He slid his finger down to a wavy ring that, in some impossible-to-describe way, just seemed really annoying.

". . . Snivel, for whiny kids, Precocia, for kids who grow up too fast, Lipptor for kids who sass back, Sadia for really, really mean kids, and, lastly, Dupli-City for dirty, two-faced snitches."

Milton turned toward Virgil, the flashlight beam shining in his chubby face.

"My sister," Milton said with a gentle sadness. "Even though she's the reason I ended up here, I can't just leave her behind."

Milton's eyes teared up. He took off his glasses and wiped a tear away, creating a smudgy streak across his filthy face.

"Pull yourself together," said Virgil with a reassuring pat that left a hand-shaped patch of brown sludge on Milton's back. "There's probably a way to get her once we're back home, somehow," he said unconvincingly.

Milton rose, smacking his head on the top of the slimy tunnel. "Do you have any brothers or sisters?" he asked.

Virgil shook his head. "Nope. My parents said that I was perfect, so why bother having another? Though the fact that I was sixteen pounds at birth might have had something to do with it."

"Well," said Milton. "Having a sibling is . . . complicated. It's like you're two prisoners handcuffed together through life. Half the time you want to strangle each other, and the other half . . . Well, okay, maybe you want to strangle them almost *all* of the time, but still: they are a part of you, and even though you dream about being apart, you can't really imagine it, know what I mean?"

Again Virgil shook his head.

Milton sighed. "Blood is thicker than logic, I guess. All I know is that I'm not leaving without her."

Virgil grumbled. "We just don't have time. The second they notice we're gone, they'll drag us back here faster than you can say 'The devil made me do it.' "

Virgil turned the map back over to the intricate diagram of Limbo's sewage pipes.

"And Heck is bad enough," he added. "I can only imagine what their idea of 'extra punishment' is."

Virgil looked into Milton's sad eyes and sighed.

"Besides, how bad can Heck be for a girl, anyway?"

21 · SUGAR, SPICE, AND EVERYTHING MEAN

THE FIRST TEN seconds of freedom Marlo enjoyed after setting off the water alarm were thrilling. Amazing. Exhilarating. Unfortunately, they also happened to be her *last* ten seconds of freedom.

"Guardettes!" Miss Borden bellowed from around the bend.

Marlo had been alone when pulling the alarm. Almost immediately the hallway was full of frantic girls running for their afterlives. Unfortunately, Marlo always had a fascination for seeing how her acts of mischief played out, which often left her rooted to the scene of the crime. Similarly unfortunate for Lyon and Bordeaux, the two girls felt themselves too cool for running. They came sauntering into the hall well after the initial wave of commotion.

Miss Borden stormed around the corner from home ec on her way to the teachers' lounge. Almost immediately upon hearing Miss Borden's shriek, decaying she-demons surrounded the three girls left in the hallway.

"One of you must be guilty," the teacher accused as she dug her squeaky leather heels into the floor, stopping dead in front of the girls. "Perhaps all of you, in some kind of conspiracy. But when did you find time to hatchet—um, hatch it?"

The girls stared blankly at Miss Borden, which was particularly easy for Bordeaux as that was her usual way of staring. The trio suddenly began accusing each other at once.

"It was Marlo—"

"It was Lyon—"

"It was—"

"I don't have time to split hairs!" the teacher barked, folding her arms against her chest. "Especially when there are parts I would much *prefer* to split. Guardettes, bring these girls to the showers!"

The guardettes promptly herded the trio of sooty girls to their pre-punishment cleaning. Heck may not have graded on a curve, Marlo thought, but it certainly punished on one. Even though she was *way* guilty, the injustice of it all just *bugged* her—of course, not to the point of actually stepping forward and confessing.

But here in the girls' showers she would come clean nonetheless. She could use a good shower, Marlo thought, with clouds of delicious, fragrant steam curling up and around her.

The trio were stripped down and pitchspork-prodded to the shower stalls. A gnarled she-demon turned a corroded metal wheel and a vicious torrent of sand and bitter cold air shot out of the three spigots. The girls screamed as they were rubbed raw by the abrasive arctic blast.

When the frigid sandstorm finally ceased, the girls were thrown stiff, stained towels. They painfully wiped away clots of caked sand from their tender, stinging skin.

At the next stall over, Bordeaux shook a small desert out of her bleached hair. "I am going to need, like, *so* much conditioner," she whined.

Bordeaux turned toward Marlo and stared like a bored cat that had just spied a twitching mouse. "Hey! No boys allowed in the shower, perv," she smirked.

Marlo exhumed a clod of grit from her ear.

"What?" she replied.

Lyon, tall, lean, and so flawless that she scarcely looked human, stood just outside the shower stalls.

"You've got a couple of zits on your chest, perv," she said icily, pointing to Marlo's underdeveloped upper body. "I guess you ran out of room on your face."

The two girls cackled. Marlo touched her cheek. It felt like chocolate chip cookie dough, heavy on the chips.

Marlo's face turned red. Her blush throbbed. Humiliated, she quickly wrapped herself in a towel and ran off as the cruel blond goddesses laughed at her. Their hoots and howls echoed off the wet tiles.

"Nice try with the water alarm," Lyon snorted.

"I don't think Miss *Boredom* appreciated it, though," Bordeaux added.

"But I'm sure you two can bury the hatchet during your detention!"

"Enough!" barked a she-demon from the hallway. "This is a strictly No Joy Zone."

Marlo wept silently in front of a mirror as her tormentors giggled quietly in the other room. Wiping her puffy, red-rimmed eyes, Marlo caught her reflection. Her face, much to her shock, was covered with pimples that formed the shape of an upside-down star. Marlo clutched her cheeks, feeling so ugly that she half expected her reflection to crack before her very eyes.

Suddenly the mirror shattered into a hundred pieces.

Marlo gasped.

A filthy head peered back through the broken mirror. If this was a demon, Marlo thought, it certainly was one of the lesser demons. Actually, it looked a lot like her brother.

"It's me, Milton!" Her brother extended a dirty hand. "C'mon! We don't have much time!"

Marlo's zit-studded face was slack with shock. "How did you find me?"

"We got a map," Milton panted. "The girls' and boys' bathrooms share the same plumbing. We're off to find the Secret Toilet."

"We?" Marlo peered inside the putrid tunnel just beyond the broken mirror. *"The Secret Toilet?"* Have you lost your mind?"

"We have to hurry," Milton whined. "She'll be looking for us . . . Principal Bubb."

At the sound of the demoness's name, Marlo clutched her towel around her and carefully crawled through the jagged portal. "And to think, I just took a shower."

Despite the stench, it was comforting to see her brother's dorky face.

"This better be worth it, short bus," she complained.

Having a brother was weird, Marlo pondered, unconsciously echoing her brother's earlier thought. It was like having a heart-shaped bruise.

22 · THE FLUSH OF YOUTH

MILTON, MARLO, AND Virgil trudged through the humid darkness. Milton and Virgil's flashlights flickered before them, with Virgil's beam often resting on Marlo.

Marlo sighed. "A little more light in front and less behind, Supersize," she grumbled.

"My flashlight must be, uh, falling off my head or something," stammered Virgil.

"Yeah, well, your big noggin is going to fall off if you keep staring at my butt."

"Hey, give him a break," Milton protested. "His map helped us find the Girls' Unrestrooms. And maybe it can help us find this Secret Toilet."

"I'll believe it when I see it," Marlo snorted, shaking her head.

Milton stared at his sister, the beam of his flashlight

caressing her fresh crop of acne. "What's that all over your face?"

Marlo went from brash to bashful. "It's, uh, a hormonal thing," she replied, brushing her hair into her face. "A *girl thing*. If you don't stop bugging me about it, I'll tell you."

The tunnel echoed with a low grumble. Marlo looked back at Virgil. She scowled at him.

Virgil glanced ahead, worried. "That wasn't me."

The three children stared down the tunnel into the impenetrable darkness. It rumbled like the irritable bowels of a giant who had just eaten a ton of spicy Chinese takeout.

Milton screamed as several tons of sewage exploded into the tunnel.

23 · FROM MALL RATS
TO SEWER RATS

ON THE SURFACE, Milton thought, people are always talking about how there is a "light at the end of the tunnel." But the only thing at the end of this particular tunnel was tons of sewage. And every ounce of it had swept him, his sister, and his new friend miles down a subterranean poop chute.

"Wow," mumbled Virgil, his face slick with stinking muck. "That was one wild ride!"

The surge of sewage had blasted the fugitive three-some through miles and miles of uncharted pipe. They were spun around so much in waves of waste they had no idea which end was up. Marlo clutched her once merely dirty towel with one arm, while the other wrapped around a rusty metal ladder welded to the inside of the pipe. Apart from the appalling smell, she looked as if she had just emerged from a therapeutic mud bath at some expensive spa.

"Second to that church summer camp Mom and Dad made us go to, that was the most disgusting thing I've ever experienced," Marlo said through clenched teeth.

Milton didn't answer. He was clinging to the ladder, paralyzed by disgust. Virgil was a few rungs below. He wiped away thick globs of crud from his eyes and consulted his map, which was now, basically, a piece of used toilet paper.

"I think we're here," he said, pointing to a patch of brown on the back of the slimy map that illustrated a dense network of pipes, tubes, and channels.

Marlo knelt beside Virgil, who stared at her, grinning like an idiot.

"Oh yeah," she said sarcastically, squinting at the map. "We're just a few turds away from home. All we have to do is turn left at the reeking dung heap."

Virgil snickered. "You're funny."

Marlo smirked at her rotund traveling companion. She was both highly irritated and strangely touched at being Virgil's crush.

Marlo examined the bottom of the map and scratched away a film of filth with her fingernail, revealing the words "Netherworld Novelty Corp." She gave a dry, humorless laugh and wiped away a budding tear.

"Figures . . . a big fat practical joke . . . on us."

Virgil gazed at Marlo with a hurt expression. She put her dirty hand on his dirty shoulder.

"Not you. You're just gullible."

Marlo looked over at her brother, who was still shaky from what would be known from then on only as "the incident." He seemed like a newborn foal, trembling and swaying and slick with feces.

"Hey, freak show . . . short bus . . . *Milton.*"

Milton gasped for air, as if he had risen to the surface of the ocean. Marlo put her hand on his shivering shoulder.

"Whoa, get a grip, geek," she said while wiping some grime from Milton's one lens. "We'll get you a nice, hot shower and a series of allergy shots when we're outta here. Promise. Cross my heart and hope to die again."

The animal-formerly-known-as-Cerberus, ferreted away in Milton's backpack, sneezed and squirmed. Milton snapped out of his stupor and looked down the putrid pipe.

"Which . . . way?" he muttered.

"Huh?" Virgil grunted as he tried to right himself in the slick puddles of waste.

Milton opened his mouth, but, instead of words, out came a few half-digested Brussels sprouts and liver lumps.

"Charming." Marlo grimaced.

"Where the sewage . . . s-somewhere up there . . . ," Milton stammered, his quivering finger pointing at the blackness ahead. "If all this . . . stuff . . . came from the Surface, the Stage, the place we call home, then it would only make sense to follow the pipe . . . *upstream*."

"What about that Secret Toilet of yours?" asked Marlo. "Shouldn't we go back to finding that?"

Milton shook his head.

"We've washed away too . . . too far." He coughed. "We'd spend most of our time backtracking to where we came from."

"And," said Virgil as he sloshed toward the Fausters. "If all this stuff goes down to . . . the hot place . . . to make it even worse, I guess . . ."

Milton shuddered at the thought.

". . . then," Virgil continued, "we could get washed down to h-e-double-hockey-sticks."

The three children shared a moment of silence.

"Well," Marlo said abruptly, "then we'd better hurry and hope we get . . . wherever . . . before the next big flush."

Cerberus poked his nose out of Milton's bag and took in a big, stinky drink of air. His eyes gave off a faint red glimmer as he scanned the pipeway dutifully. Milton reached back and gave what he thought was his ferret a reassuring pat. "What's up, little guy?"

The creature hissed.

"Is he okay?" Virgil asked.

Milton looked around with dread. "I'm not sure. He hasn't been himself lately. Maybe he senses danger."

"I don't think you have to be a ferret to sense *that*," Marlo added bleakly.

24 · PIPE DREAM COME TRUE

AFTER HOURS OF slogging through filth, Milton had all but given up hope. Heck was creeping into Milton's skin. A sense of despair had taken root within him.

Yet, as they trudged through the sludge, Milton spotted a weak beam of light glimmering ahead. His heart, had it been beating, would surely have stopped at the sight. Perhaps they'd soon be waking from this nightmare, he thought. Although the realist in Milton persisted: maybe this was just another dirty trick.

At the end of the passageway was a ceiling grate. Faint beams of light trickled through.

Virgil grinned like a cat that had just eaten a flock of canaries.

"Wow," said Marlo. "I'm impressed. You really did it, Superchunk."

Virgil blushed. "Ladies first," he said with a sly smile. "Just get on my shoulders and crawl through."

Marlo stepped forward, clutching the soggy towel wrapped around her, then stopped short. Her eyes squeezed into accusing slits.

"Nice try, perv. Milton, *you* go first."

"Why me?"

"Because I said so," Marlo responded matter-of-factly.

"Oh," Milton replied meekly. Marlo wasn't the most logical person, but she made a strong argument nonetheless.

Desperate to emerge from this long metal intestine, Milton crawled onto Virgil's shoulders. He lifted the grate and peered out.

"So?" Virgil asked. "Did we make it?"

"Yes," Milton answered with a mixture of delight and suspicion. "Maybe. At least I . . . think."

The grate proved to be a manhole in the middle of a vast tunnel clogged with honking cars.

Milton helped pull Virgil through the manhole while Marlo, much to her disgust, pushed. Virgil's face was purple from exertion. He looked like a distant cousin of that annoying purple dinosaur down below . . . or above . . . or to the side . . . or wherever the heck they were. It sure *looked* like they were back home.

"C'mon," strained Milton as sweat poured down his face. "One more time . . . One, two, *three!*"

Virgil popped out of the hole like a humongous cork in a champagne bottle of questionable vintage. Marlo struggled upward as Virgil pulled her by her arm.

"Oww," she whined while planting herself on the asphalt. "You, baby, definitely have *back*."

Virgil smiled, happy for any acknowledgment, and the three of them rose, steadying themselves against the oversized tires of a gargantuan SUV with a "Looking Out for Me, Myself, and I" sticker on its mangled bumper.

They walked down a seemingly endless row of cars. Behind the wheel of each was an angry, cursing commuter.

"It's like it never ends," Virgil said while staring at an old woman smashing her fist on the dashboard, knocking over a small plastic Jesus. "And they don't seem to even see us."

Marlo winced as the woman laid on her horn. "How come we didn't hear any of this in the sewage pipe?"

Milton shrugged. "Maybe there's some kind of sound insulation field or something."

Marlo shook her head. "I don't know. The whole thing is just weird."

All the drivers were staring straight ahead at a bright light at the end of the tunnel. It was round, like a spotlight, radiating a pure white beam. There was movement around the edges, indistinct figures. It looked as if they were beckoning the drivers toward them. The three children squinted at the light trying to make sense of it.

"So *that* was the light we saw in the pipe," Milton said.

They continued onward and passed a dented silver BMW. Inside a businessman fumed.

"Move it! I'm late!!" he screamed. "Where'd you learn how to drive—clown school?"

Virgil chortled. "Good one."

Milton saw a cell phone on the man's dashboard. "Excuse me, sir? Do you mind if I borrow your phone?" Milton asked.

The businessman ignored him. On his radio a monotone announcer droned.

"This is a test of the Emergency Broadcast System. This is only a test."

A piercing tone blasted from the speakers. It streamed from each and every car on this endless stretch of road. Marlo grabbed the phone through the man's half-open window.

"I'll take that as a yes," she said.

She flipped the phone open and punched in a number. Someone on the other end picked up.

"Mom?!" Marlo said with a blend of desperation and excitement.

"You are trying to place a call way, way out of your cellular phone network," replied a flat, prerecorded female voice. *"My, we must think our calling plan grants us the ability to traverse both time and space. Didn't you read your terms and conditions? Apparently not. Please stay on the line. An operator will be with you shortly. Estimated time of wait: forever."*

"Is it her?" Milton asked, trembling.

Marlo sniffed back an unexpected tear. Milton gazed up at her in confused anticipation. Marlo turned away suddenly.

"Allergies," she snuffled. She wiped away some snot with the back of her hand and tossed the phone back into the grumbling man's car.

Milton tugged on Marlo's towel.

"Well?" he asked, scooting in front of her.

"Out of range," she continued with a couldn't-care-less shrug.

Milton scrutinized his sister. She appeared nonchalant on the outside. But he could tell by how hard she was *trying* to appear nonchalant on the outside that, inside, she must be a mess. A cold chill ran up his spine. Wherever they were, Milton surmised, they were still a long, long way from home.

A big book rested on the seat next to the man: *Contract Law Made EZ*. There was something about the book that captured Milton's attention. Sure, it was probably pretty boring, but if they hadn't really made it back home—and, judging from how hard Marlo was trying to look casual, that was probably the case—it could very well hold the key to breaking his contract with Bea "Elsa" Bubb. Besides, it was something to read, and when Milton was stressed out (and he thought that dying and being sentenced to eternal torment were valid reasons for feeling stressed) reading anything—old magazines, cereal boxes, the ingredients on a tube of toothpaste, whatever he could get his hands on—had a calming effect on him.

"Hey, mister. Do you mind if . . . ?"

The man, oblivious, was locked tight inside his road rage. Milton grabbed a notebook from his backpack, ripped out a page, and wrote "I.O.U. one law book."

He folded the page, placed it on the passenger seat, and stuffed the book into his backpack.

"Look!" Virgil yelped.

He pointed toward a wide pile of jagged shadows several hundred feet down the tunnel, where the rows of idle cars seemed to end abruptly. A blazing beam of white light emanated from just beyond it. The light stroked the gloom in slow sweeps. The tunnel grew steadily wider until reaching a massive, darkened barricade.

Milton, Marlo, and Virgil jogged through the traffic jam toward the line of shadows. With each step, it became clearer that this dark blockage was a gnarled hedge of wrecked cars and that the light itself was nothing but a high-powered klieg light with a buzzing bluish white bulb. Squinting, they could make out that the gesturing figures in front of the light were animatronic robots: jerky, humanoid machines dressed as old men and women. It was like they had stumbled upon a movie premiere at a rest home.

The barricade of cars girdled a massive concrete wall, camouflaged by black paint, which seemed to signify the end of the tunnel.

The three children considered the forbidding piles of neglected cars, some with headlights slowly dying into weak yellow-orange embers.

"Here!" Marlo shouted as she opened the door of a mangled '63 T-bird. She crawled through it and came out next to the towering rampart.

After Virgil and Milton followed Marlo through the car, Milton walked up to the wall. It was the side of a massive building that seemed to him both ancient and modern, like it had either been new for thousands of years, or was built old just yesterday. Milton noticed a shabby billboard posted on the wall several yards to his left. Etched in the pockmarked sign—surrounded by smeared graffiti scrawls—were the letters DURBR.

Virgil peered behind the light as Marlo made shadow birds in front with her hands. Her sweeping eagle, in particular, was received with an explosion of honks and screams from the traffic jam.

"I found a door!" Virgil shouted from beneath the DURBR sign, his hand on the tarnished knob of a dull charcoal door.

So the three not-quite children, not-quite teenagers stepped through the door into a place that seemed not-quite home, not-quite Heck.

25 · WAIT WATCHERS

THEY ENTERED A sprawling gray building. It was a huge square room lined with counters, most of which had little signs that read CLOSED. TRY NEXT TELLER. GOOD LUCK WITH THAT. Lines of people with drooped shoulders, shifting their weight restlessly from foot to foot, stood vigilantly in front of the few tellers actually at their post.

The air had that same dead quality that Milton noticed in chemistry class mixed with the odor of old carpet, mildew, dust, and despair. The whole place just *smelled* gray.

Rows of morose adults slumped in folding metal chairs, gazing dismally at the ticket stubs in their hands.

The only feeble splash of atmospheric color in this place came in the form of cheery music squawking through speakers embedded in the crumbling asbestos ceiling.

Up, up and away, my beautiful, my beautiful balloon . . .

A huge, run-down metal sign displaying a long row of numbers clicked loudly. A new number dropped slowly into place like a glob of cold ketchup creeping out of an upended bottle.

NOW SERVING: 5,769,343,782,312.

One disheveled man in a trench coat held up his ticket in disbelief. "5,769,343,782,312? That's me!"

The man shuffled across the carpet to a lumpy woman behind a counter. She was chewing gum. Gobs of it. Her jaws chomped in listless rhythm and caused her three chins to sway back and forth. She resembled a cow with gray hair and beige stirrup pants. The man knocked on her window just as she flipped her sign to CLOSED. She waved her painted, dagger-like nails toward the counter next to her, where several hundred people fidgeted in line.

The sign clicked again: NOW SERVING: 5,769,343,782,313.

The second clerk shrugged her padded shoulders. "Sorry, sir. You missed your turn. You'll have to wait."

The world's a nicer place in my beautiful balloon . . .

The man plodded back to his chair in defeat as Milton knocked on the cow lady's window. She ignored him in that "pretending not to notice you" kind of way. Marlo stepped forward.

"Hey! Lady!"

The woman looked up reluctantly. She squinted at Marlo through cat's-eye glasses. A glimmer of recognition flashed in her dull eyes.

"You three look . . ." She thrummed her stiletto fingernails on the counter. "I'll get my supervisor to help you. Wait here . . . *Ha*, like you could do anything else."

She pushed three long sheets of paper across the counter. "In the meantime, please fill out these Capture forms . . . Be sure to sign the back, people always forget to do that."

She shut her window and waddled toward a bank of offices behind her.

Marlo noticed an engraved wooden sign above the windows of the counter: DEPARTMENT OF UNENDURABLE REDUNDANCY, BUREAUCRACY, AND REDUNDANCY. She swallowed hard.

Way up in the air in my beautiful balloon . . .

"We're done here, boys," Marlo said with a quaver, pushing the forms back across the counter.

Milton, Marlo, and Virgil pushed through the lines of people to a revolving door at the back of the room. Through the door was a winding white corridor, like a hospital hallway, with a rainbow of colored bands on the gray linoleum floor that branched out in a dozen directions.

"Well," Marlo said, beginning to run, "I've always been partial to purple."

They dashed along the plum-colored line, which veered sharply to the right. Milton looked over his shoulder. Three withered demon guards with matching shocks of gray hair struggled through the revolving doors behind them. Once free, they bounded toward the three children with surprising speed.

If you'll hold my hand, we'll chase your dream across the sky, for we can fly . . .

"I don't know what's worse," Marlo said, panting as she galloped down the hallway, "being chased by demons or that awful music . . . it's everywhere."

Virgil wheezed. "I . . . kind of . . . like it . . . *sort of* . . . It's very . . . *relaxing* . . ."

Marlo clutched her soiled towel.

"Figures," she puffed. "It's like a musical lobotomy."

Up, up and away, my beautiful, my beautiful balloon . . .

The purple line ended at a like-colored double door. Hanging on the twin doorknobs was a cardboard sign on a string, reading DO NOT DISTURB: TIME-OUT.

Marlo pulled off the sign and threw open the doors.

Milton, Marlo, and Virgil burst into a vast windowless space lined with shiny gray linoleum. Hundreds of agitated young children with cones on their heads twitched in folding metal chairs that faced the walls.

An old woman who looked like a puckered praying mantis paced the room, smacking a yardstick in her palm.

"Now stop all that blubbering!" she scolded. "You only have to stay here until the cows come home, or the place downstairs freezes, whichever comes last!"

Milton, Marlo, and Virgil closed the door behind them as quietly as possible. Unfortunately, they stuck out like three giant, soiled thumbs.

The withered insect lady glared at the three filthy preteens.

"You're a little old for this place, aren't you?"

Marlo stepped forward and cinched her towel tightly beneath her underarms.

"We have overactive thyroids," Marlo declared. Then, with her usual grace and subtlety, she added, "Tell us where we are."

"Take a seat," the teacher spat. "You'll have plenty of time to figure it out."

Milton walked toward a group of vacant chairs in the middle of the wall opposite them.

"I'm starting to think we might not be home," whispered Virgil next to him.

I sort of figured that once I saw the battalion of decomposing demons after us, Milton thought.

He studied the room. There were no other doors, no

other way out. The room was still except for the occasional whimper or squirming limb. From down the hall Milton could hear grumbling and doors opening and shutting.

Virgil stared at the double doors.

"This isn't going to work," he said. "They're going to find us. We've got to find another way out of here."

"Shhhhh!!" the sour teacher hissed.

"There isn't," Milton said hopelessly.

Marlo scanned the room like a caged animal.

"Wait," she yelped. "Up there!"

The ceiling was tiled in big, dingy white squares. One of the tiles was askew. A warm, faint light shone through the gap.

"I smell cookies," Virgil said, sniffing up great gulps of air.

Marlo scooted a chair underneath it and hopped on top.

"I . . . can't . . . quite . . . reach," she said, teetering on her tiptoes.

"We'll have to get on top of each other or something," Milton commented beside her.

He looked over at Virgil and considered his bulk. "Due to our unique . . . body types, maybe you should be the bottom, while we climb on top."

The shriveled teacher held a bony finger to her mouth. "Shhhhh!!!" she said with an explosive spray of spit. "Sit down this instant!!"

Marlo looked at Virgil.

"Only problem with that," she said, "is that we'd have to, somehow, pull him up."

Virgil shrugged his shoulders apologetically.

"Good point," Milton said while rubbing his chin in contemplation. "Well, here goes . . ."

Milton scaled his sister, trying to touch her as little as possible.

"You could at least take off those stupid wooden shoes," Marlo grumbled.

The teacher glowered at them, dumbfounded, with her withered arms on her hips. "What on earth do you wretched children think you're doing!? Come down from there!"

Marlo groaned as Milton ascended her. "We're not *on* earth," she grunted. "That's the problem, bone bag."

Securely on her shoulders, Milton managed to push the tile aside. "Close . . . Virgil, you're up."

The teacher was livid. You could see the anger pulsing along her network of bulging blue veins. She stormed at Milton, Marlo, and Virgil, waving her yardstick.

The Fausters moaned in agony as their full-bodied friend climbed to the top of their living totem pole. Finally, after much wheezing and mumbled curses, Virgil made it to the top.

He poked his head in. "Wow," he murmured, "you're not going to believe this."

Marlo was sweating under the strain. "And you're

not going to believe my chiropractor bill if you don't get off me!"

"Oh," Virgil mumbled, "sorry."

The double doors of the classroom rattled open. Several pairs of hard leather jackboots slapped the floor below. Virgil crawled into the ceiling and grabbed Milton's arm.

"Whoa!" Virgil yelled as he suddenly fell *into* the ceiling, pulling both Milton and Marlo in as well.

They fell onto the floor of a child's bedroom. The hole in the ceiling of the room below—or at least it seemed as if it were below—had led to a hole behind a black velvet snowman painting hanging on a wall in *this* room. It defied the laws of physics and gravity. But obviously whoever had made those laws had never spent time down here.

26 · ALWAYS WINTER, NEVER CHRISTMAS

A LITTLE BOY sat on a bed, clutching his knees. Across from him was another bed covered with pink stuffed unicorns, on which a little girl—wide awake—shook back and forth excitedly.

"Hello!" said the trembling little girl, who looked like she was about to wet her bed.

Marlo and Milton stared at each other.

"Where are we?" Milton asked.

"You're in our bedroom, silly," the little girl replied. "What do you think Santa is going to bring you?"

"Santa?" Virgil said, reaching instinctively for a half-eaten cupcake on the boy's bedside table. "There isn't any . . ."

Marlo nudged Virgil in the ribs with her elbow—no easy feat.

"What do you mean?" asked Milton.

"Christmas!" shrieked the little boy and girl. "It's almost Christmas! Look!"

The little girl pointed at a snowman clock on the wall, framed by twinkling Christmas lights. The clock read "11:59."

Milton was filled with a strange electricity. This cheery room made him feel happy and warm inside. But it wasn't your standard-issue kind of joy. It was joy with an edge. Happiness with a hunger to it, an appetite that ached, that could never be filled. It crackled all around him, making him itchy and agitated. It was like when he waited in line to see *The Lord of the Rings*. It was exciting, yet it gave him an ulcer. If he felt any merrier, he would explode.

"Lucky" chose that moment to poke his white fuzzy head out of Milton's backpack, sniff the air, and bound out of the bag.

"Oh boy!" yelped the little boy. "A weasel! Just what I always wanted!"

The counterfeit ferret crawled toward a glass of milk and a plate of cookies on the girl's nightstand.

"He's *not* a weasel," said Milton defensively. "He's a ferret. And he's mine."

"Hey!" the little girl shouted. "That milk is for Santa!"

The creature looked up from the milk and hissed.

Milton looked at the clock on the wall: 11:59.

Virgil wiped frosting from his lower lip and whispered to Milton. "It's been 11:59 for a while now."

"Maybe the clock is broken," said Marlo.

"No," Virgil replied. "The second hand keeps moving around; it just never gets to midnight."

"Always winter, never Christmas," murmured Milton.

"Huh?" asked Marlo.

"It's from a book," he replied. "Never mind."

"It's like we traded one Limbo for another," Virgil muttered weakly.

"And another, and another . . . ," added Marlo.

"Hey!" the little boy screamed. "Stop!"

The not-so-Lucky, with a frosted reindeer cookie in his mouth (Rudolph with a cinnamon Red Hot for a nose), leapt off the table and scurried out of the room.

"Lucky! Wait!" Milton screeched as he ran after him.

"You can't go down yet," wailed the little girl. "IT'S NOT TIME!"

Cerberus, in his ferret suit, rippled down the stairs like a fuzzy white Slinky, the glazed Rudolph still clutched in his jaws.

Milton rushed after him. Marlo started to follow, but, as she passed the clock on the wall, she began to twitch. It was what happened when she saw something she was about to steal. An itch she had to scratch. As she, with her near-legendary light touch, plucked the clock from the wall, the word "evidence" popped into her head. Her thoughts were tugged back to Ms. Mallon's class. With any crime, you needed to collect evidence to support your case. If anything was a crime, it was this place, and she felt sure her brother would think of something. He always did.

So she tucked the clock beneath her arm and descended the stairs into a living room decked out in magical Christmas finery. It looked like an explosion at a tinsel factory. Twinkling lights in a rainbow of colors, candy-cane candles flickering, battery-operated snowmen waving . . . and in the middle of it all, a massive pine tree—twenty feet tall at least—surrounded by heaps of presents lavishly wrapped with green and red bows.

It was painfully beautiful. It was almost enough to make a jaded kid believe in Santa all over again. But there was something about the festive scene that made Milton uncomfortable. It was too perfect. Cruelly so.

The fake ferret rushed toward the largest gift under the tree, then suddenly stopped in his tracks. He dropped the cookie and sniffed the box with abandon, baring his needle-like teeth into something like a smile.

"What is it, little guy?" Marlo asked, stooping next to him.

Just then the oversized box shuddered.

Milton instinctively scooped up his pet. "Don't worry," he said. "I've got you."

The fuzzy imposter squirmed and spat, wanting nothing more than to get back to the box.

"He's really upset," Milton said. "This is all probably too much for him."

Milton stuffed the twitching animal deep into his knapsack, then strapped it shut. The sack quivered and quaked as "Lucky" desperately fought to get out.

Milton took a deep breath and approached the trembling package.

"Stop!" screamed the little girl from the top of the stairs. Both she and her brother acted as if there was an invisible force field preventing them from descending. They shook with both fear and excitement. Their hair stood on end.

"You can't open a present before Christmas!" the little boy yelled desperately. "You'll spoil everything!"

Virgil slogged past them down the stairs. The terrified children gawked, as if he had just jumped off a cliff.

"I don't like this," Marlo murmured as she wrapped her arms around herself and shivered.

The box convulsed anew. Virgil pushed the Fauster children aside, stepping defiantly toward the present.

"It's okay," he said. "I'm Jewish. I'll be fine."

Virgil bent down. Up close, the green and red foil and silver silk bow looked somehow sinister. The quivering box was both wonderful and wicked, like a chocolate-covered jalapeño.

Virgil examined the tangle of ribbon as if defusing a

bomb, cautiously gauging which wire to cut. He gave the bow a tug. Suddenly a long black claw stabbed through the "gift" from the inside.

Virgil jumped back and fell on his substantial backside.

The little boy and girl craned their necks to see.

"Is that Santa Claus?" the girl asked timidly.

Virgil, Milton, and Marlo stared bug-eyed as the gift began to unwrap itself.

"Whoever's claws those are," muttered Virgil, "they sure as heck ain't Santa's."

His curiosity getting the best of him, Milton inched toward the gift.

With a great pop, the box's lid shot off like a rocket, hitting the ceiling. The gift wrapping shred into a cloud of glittering confetti and the lofty, lavishly decorated pine tree toppled as Bea "Elsa" Bubb climbed out of the box.

Towering over the threesome, Bea "Elsa" Bubb pulled a large can of Not-So-Silly String from her purse.

"This is going to hurt you much, much more than it will me," she said with a sneer.

She sprayed the trembling escapees, coating them thoroughly with yards and yards of gooey, multicolored ribbons. The candy-colored cocoon stiffened into a hard, unyielding shell, with Milton, Marlo, and Virgil sealed inside.

27 · TO HECK IN A HANDBASKET

THE ELEVATOR—MORE like an oversized wicker hamper— shook, clacked, and squealed its way down . . . or up . . . or across. It was hard to tell when you were wrapped up like a mummy.

In the darkness Milton bobbed in and out of consciousness. He could only imagine what kind of punishment Bea "Elsa" Bubb had in store for him. What could she possibly dish out that could be worse than simply going back to Heck—that is, if they had ever truly left?

The suffocating heat inside the Not-So-Silly String shell sent him back inside his feverish brain.

Milton was in his bed. He rose and stretched, comforted by his familiar surroundings. Something troubled him, however. He looked at the lump next to him beneath the sheet. He ripped off the sheet and lying beside him was Marlo, physically attached to him like a Siamese twin. They gaped at each other in horror and screamed.

Milton came to in the dark shell, screaming. Marlo was wedged into his left side (luckily not permanently), while Virgil woke up on his right.

Phew, Milton thought. *Just a dream. No Siamese twin. Just me, encased in thick plastic strings, imprisoned by a demoness in the underworld.*

Virgil's eyes bulged from their sockets in sheer panic.

"Where . . . what . . . I'M FREAKING OUT!" Virgil flailed in vain trying to escape from the hard Not-So-Silly String coating.

"Oww!" yelped Marlo as she was squeezed awake by Virgil's fit. She stole a look through a crack in the shell.

Next to them Bea "Elsa" Bubb sighed and stared at the elevator wall as it blinked its journey: Snivel, Fibble, Blimpo, Rapacia. She grudgingly scraped away a patch of crusty string from the children's heads.

"Yuck!" Milton spat out a glob of green and yellow string. "What—*where* were we?"

"You mean Candyland, Oz, the mythical Secret Toilet?" the principal laughed.

Marlo shot Virgil an "I *so* told you so" look. Milton sighed and shook his head as much as he could.

"No, the tunnel, the Department of Unendurable Redundancy and . . . *whatever* . . . the classroom with all the chairs . . . the almost-Christmas house . . ."

Bea "Elsa" Bubb rolled her lizard eyes as she jabbed the elevator button with her claw.

"The Department of Unendurable Redundancy, Bureaucracy, and Redundancy," she said with fatigue, "just off the Netherworld Distressway. It's where all the paperwork in the netherworld goes to get sorted, filed, and ultimately misplaced, part of our Purgatory While-U-Wait project. Now, as we continue our descent, please return your nasty trap to its original, sealed-shut position before I shut it for you."

"But what about—" Milton continued.

"What part of 'shut up' don't you understand?" the principal snapped. "The netherworld is a vast and complicated place. Did you think that the little corner of it you saw was all there was, you self-centered little twerp?"

If Milton wanted answers, he knew he'd have to try a different approach. He thought about all those goofy spy movies where the evil villain felt compelled to tell the hero absolutely every detail of his dastardly plan out of arrogance and pride. Milton decided to play to Bea "Elsa" Bubb's vanity.

"It's just that I find this whole place fascinating, Principal Bubb," Milton said sweetly. "How you can keep track of everything. I mean . . . *wow.*"

Principal Bubb considered Milton suspiciously before ultimately falling prey to the quicksand of flattery.

"Well," she replied awkwardly, "it really . . . you get used to it. It's not easy. In fact, it's the hardest job you'll ever loathe."

"What about the place with the chairs?" Marlo interjected while trying vainly to wriggle out of her crunchy coating.

"And the Christmas house," Milton chimed in.

"Time-out," Bea "Elsa" Bubb replied, rubbing her temples as if she were trying to subdue a migraine that had been festering in her head for the last century, give or take a decade. "Where impulsive, not-too-bad, not-too-good toddlers go until they are reintroduced to the Surface. Time-out and Purgatory While-U-Wait are basically collections of moments strung together in infinite loops. States of mind more than physical places."

"How innovative," Milton said.

The principal's ample chest heaved with self-satisfaction.

"Yes," she answered with a grin, "an idea that I, if I may humbly add, conjured one morning while sitting on the . . ."

The beastly demoness coughed.

"Anyway," Bea "Elsa" Bubb continued, "instead of wasting surreal estate on cells for our temporary guests, we just carve out desperately dull moments, slice them thin, and tie their ends together, seamlessly, so that they are perpetual instances: little curls of time that simply never begin or end. They just *are*. It's very economical. We save a lot on overhead, not to mention enjoy some significant tax breaks."

The elevator buzzer rang and the basket slowed to a stop.

"There's no place like homeroom . . . ," she clucked.

Milton looked at his demonic headmistress nervously. "I suppose that being sent back here is punishment enough, right?" he asked hopefully.

"Of course," Bea "Elsa" Bubb replied with a dry, disingenuous chuckle. She reached inside the sticky, multicolored shell and patted Milton on his backpack. He shivered, though her gesture was actually just a guise to slip Cerberus a succulent lump of foie gras she had tucked into her sleeve.

"In fact," she continued, "I want to reward you three for helping to find the holes in our security system."

Milton wanted to believe her, but his gut had trouble swallowing her words. Cerberus, though, had no trouble devouring his goose liver pâté. Little did Milton know, his digestive troubles were just beginning.

28 · UNJUST DESSERTS

IT LOOKED LIKE a perfectly ordinary living room. Rather nice, actually. Big, warm, sparsely yet tastefully decorated with an overstuffed couch and a coffee table strewn with old *Deranger Rick* and *Lowlights* magazines.

Virgil and Marlo had been taken to other rooms, apparently. Milton was alone with Bea "Elsa" Bubb. She was being quite cordial. Very personable, for a nonperson. Which started to freak him out. She seemed like a grinning Venus flytrap with lipstick.

"Excuse me?" replied Milton, thinking he hadn't heard her correctly.

"I asked, dear," she cooed, "what is your favorite food?"

Hmm, thought Milton with distress. *This has to be*

some kind of trick. Surely she's not going to serve me a plate of tiramisù. She just wants me to think she's going to do something nice.

Principal Bubb's face crinkled with impatience.

Unless, Milton continued in his mind, *she wants me to think it's a trick, in which case she'd expect me to ask for my least favorite food, therefore serving me something terrible . . .*

"Please," the vile demoness grunted, her sweetness souring. "Don't make eternity seem any longer than it already is."

Milton's stomach did a somersault. He had to think quickly.

Since I don't have all the facts, Milton mused, *then I should pick something I neither hate nor love, so the only possible answer is . . .*

"Dry toast," he blurted.

Bea "Elsa" Bubb raised her bristly, centipede-like eyebrow.

"So," she stated coolly, "of all the delectable, mouthwatering foods ever created by man to dazzle the taste buds with a delicious flurry of flavor, you pick dry toast." She shrugged her shoulders. "So be it."

She clapped her claws together. Instantly, Milton's hands were tightly bound behind his back. Bea "Elsa" Bubb strutted toward the door.

"Bon appétit," she added dryly.

Milton's curiosity became too much to bear. "So

you're not going to throw me to Damian, or take my soul, or something awful like that?"

Principal Bubb grinned coldly. "I'm saving those," she said.

Just before closing the door, she clapped again. Suddenly, the entire room was crammed with dry toast. Every square inch packed tightly with lightly browned bread. Milton couldn't move. He could barely breathe.

"Forgive me for not *toasting* to your health," Bea "Elsa" Bubb said, "but you didn't have the foresight to wish for a refreshing beverage."

He felt the bread pressing against him. He had only one course of action: eat his way out, or be crushed into a crouton.

"I never, *ever* want pudding again," moaned Virgil as he lay slumped against the wall in the hallway, sticky with chocolate. Next to him stood Marlo, trembling and mortified, covered with sticky, sickly globs of color.

A door opened and out stumbled Milton, covered with crumbs, his face scraped raw. He collapsed to the ground and gasped.

"Juice . . . milk . . . fart water . . . *anything*!"

The binding around his wrists disappeared. Milton slowly stood and scrutinized his friend and sister. "Be careful what you wish for, huh?"

Virgil held his gummy head in his hands.

"It's just so . . . *mean*," he blubbered. "To make someone absolutely sick of their favorite food. Inhumane, I say. I haven't felt this awful since my parents took me to that all-you-can-eat dim-sum buffet in Las Vegas."

The boys turned to Marlo, who was uncharacteristically quiet. It made them nervous.

"What did you ask for?" Virgil asked.

Marlo looked down at her dirty feet.

"Well," she quavered, "I told the Principal of Darkness that she/it/whatever was a . . ."

She gagged and turned a peculiar shade of green.

". . . *a fruitcake*. And then, suddenly, the room was . . . full of it."

Milton winced and shook his head. He knew all too well about Marlo's *thing* with fruitcake. It represented, to her, everything that was wrong with society, baked into a cake. The stale tastelessness, the booger-like mystery fruit, the complete lack of imagination as a holiday gift . . .

"What's so bad about fruitcake?" Virgil asked innocently while wiping his mouth clean of chocolate.

Marlo cupped her mouth and forced back the wave of half-digested cake crawling up her throat.

Bea "Elsa" Bubb crept out of Punishment Pit #3— another "living room" like the one Milton had just eaten his way out of—smearing pudding on a toasted fruitcake sandwich.

"Mmmm," she moaned. The principal looked up at the three miserable youngsters. "Oh, forgive my manners," she said insincerely. "Would any of you charming children like a bite?"

Marlo almost lost it right then and there, while her brother and Virgil were so green that they could have signaled traffic onward.

"Fine, then," Principal Bubb said with a sneer. "I guess there's no accounting for taste . . ."

She snapped her claws.

"Guards!"

Three wiry, rotten-meat banana creatures of varying heights charged from the adjacent demon den. They gracelessly slid into formation before the principal and stamped their pitchsporks on the ground.

"Take the young lady to the girls' classrooms," Bea "Elsa" Bubb said. "All this gallivanting about has caused her to miss most of her second day. Tsk-tsk—Miss Borden wouldn't like that . . ."

Marlo cringed.

"Lucky for you," the principal continued, "this is her day off. But tomorrow she'll be razor-sharp and ready to attack the day, I'm sure."

She shooed them off with a flap of her claws. "Chop, chop," she snickered.

The guards grabbed Marlo. She thrashed about like a puppet having a seizure. Virgil, disturbed, softly sang a familiar little tune under his breath to calm himself.

"Up, up and away, my beautiful, my beautiful balloon . . ."

That song, thought Milton. *That annoying . . .*

Then something struck Milton. Not physically, of course, though that was entirely possible down here and often encouraged. But an idea, or the spark of one, anyway. An idea that had yet to float up, up and away . . .

As Marlo was dragged down the hall—digging her heels in stubbornly so that her feet squeaked all the way—the stolen clock fell from its hiding place in her grimy towel to the floor.

Milton rushed forward, picked up the clock, and handed it to one of the demon guards in a sly attempt to get closer to his sister.

"Here," he said, "make sure she gets this. It's a memento of her thwarted escape attempt and the terrible punishment she received as a result."

The demon, who seemed a few fries short of a Happy Meal, looked over at Bea "Elsa" Bubb for direction.

The principal shrugged her shoulders.

"Sure, whatever," she said. "A little extra psychological torture never hurt anyone."

The demon nodded vaguely and snatched the clock out of Milton's hands.

"Yes," he said sluggishly, "exactly what I was thinking. A pimento of her warted escapement!"

Milton leaned close to his sister.

"Liver," he whispered.

Marlo squished up her face in bewilderment.

"You know," he continued. "A liver note . . ."

The cloud of confusion on her face parted and a knowing smile shone through.

"Gotcha." She winked.

Bea "Elsa" Bubb furrowed her brow and trotted over to them.

"What did he say?" the principal snarled.

The tallest guard, whose face looked like a mummy's wrapped in black electrical tape, came forward. "Something about a liver note, ma'am," he said.

"No," Milton blurted quickly. "I said . . . 'Leave her alone' . . . You know, LEAVE MY SISTER ALONE!"

Principal Bubb smirked. "Of course," she said coolly. "After all, you call the shots down here. It's Milton's underworld, after all."

She sighed and strutted back toward Virgil, who was so full of chocolate pudding that his green eyes were practically brown.

"Playtime is over . . . Take her away," Bea "Elsa" Bubb ordered.

The guards dragged Marlo away, kicking, squirming, and cursing. "Oh, you want a piece of me, sock monkey?" she snarled. "Let's see if I can make you even uglier . . ."

Principal Bubb grabbed Virgil and Milton by the collars of their filthy shirts.

"Clean those devilishly handsome faces immediately, then report to your classes. You've missed most of them today, anyhow, but I'm sure there are degrading lessons to be learned nonetheless."

At least his failed attempt at escape had postponed his detention with Damian. *Who knows?* Milton mused. *Maybe it has been forgotten entirely.*

"And don't think we have forgotten your detention with Mr. Ruffino," Principal Bubb said with uncanny timing. "Our promising young man is at a HADES retreat today, but he will be back just before your sleep session. So now you have something to look forward to."

She turned to walk away.

"P-P-P-Principal?" Virgil stuttered.

Principal Bubb twisted about angrily.

"Yes, Mr. F-F-F-Farrow?"

Virgil stared down at his gloppy brown clogs, or would have if he could see past his enormous stomach.

"W-what class do we go to?"

Bea "Elsa" Bubb grinned from ear to ear. It was like a big, nasty yellow zipper had opened across her face.

"I'll give you a hint." She chuckled while curving one of her claws into a hook. "If your next class were a movie, it would be rated 'Arrrrrgh'!"

29 · YO-HO-HO AND
A BUCKET OF SPiT

"CLIMB THE ROPE, ya scurvy dog!" Blackbeard bellowed. "Dunna just hang there like a pair o' great big lacy bloomers!"

Virgil hung on to the rope with all his might. Though he was only a foot off the ground, it was still to be commended that a boy of his bulk could manage to support his weight at all.

A group of boys surrounded Virgil in a cackling circle. Squatting next to him was Blackbeard. Even crouching, the former pirate was an imposing sight. He was as big as an ox, had matchsticks braided into his hair and beard, and continually rubbed a nasty gash that encircled the entirety of his neck. He was also a complete and utter psycho.

"Aye, ya should be wearin' the hempen halter rather than climbin' it, ya great sack o' chum!" he roared. "If'n we were slicing across one of the seven seas like a cutlass through a puddle o' warm rum, you'd be havin' a date with Davy Jones, ya would! Cut yerself down, ya great beluga!"

Virgil had no idea what Blackbeard had just shrieked, but he inferred that he could now let go of the rope. He dropped down and collapsed on the splintering planks of the gym floor.

A tanned, curly-haired boy pointed at Virgil.

"Get a load of the beached whale!"

All of the other kids, except—of course—for Milton, roared with laughter.

"Yeah," Virgil wheezed. "Never . . . heard . . . that . . . before."

Milton broke out of the circle and stepped before Blackbeard, who had now risen to his full, towering height. Milton was about as tall as his teacher's wide leather belt. From this vantage point, he could see that the pirate's filthy vest was riddled with twenty or so jagged slits.

Wow, Milton thought, marveling at the dozens of scars and wounds on his teacher's body, *Blackbeard sure wasn't voted most popular.*

"What's on yer land-lousy mind, ya wee shred o' bait?" he asked, glowering down at Milton.

The boy gulped, straightened his glasses, and sucked

in a deep breath that, unfortunately, was infused with an overwhelming dead pirate aroma.

"Yes, Mr. . . . Beard," Milton managed. "I—I was wondering why we, us being dead and all, need to take physical education?"

Milton hoped that, through the posing of sweeping, multilayered questions, he could delay the next installment of Virgil's public humiliation.

Blackbeard rubbed his namesake while squinting down at Milton.

"Ya remind me o' me thirteenth wife," the pirate ruminated. "Always with the questions. Ya even look like her, with yer porcelain complexion and crow's-nest hairdo."

The boys behind Milton snickered. *Wonderful,* he thought. *The only thing worse than being teacher's pet was being teacher's spouse.*

Blackbeard shook his head free of ancient memories.

"It's *meta*physical education, ya polyp," the pirate groused. "Just because ya took leave of yer physical body, don't mean ya should get all lazy, like a drowsy manatee. It's like this . . ."

Blackbeard stomped back and forth between the hanging ropes.

Good, Milton mused. *He's off on a tangent. This should kill some time.*

"Who here amongst ya simpering scalawags felt a queer, quick ripping sensation—like lightning through a mainsail—upon yer unfortunate passage?"

The boys looked at one another awkwardly before sheepishly raising their hands. Milton *had* wondered what that painful tingle was all about. He had just chocked it up to the many things he did not know about the process of dying. But, boy, was he learning the hard way.

"Have ya miserable barnacles thought about why ya look like yerselves while yerselves are up on the Stage rotting away in a pine box?"

Again Blackbeard brought up a good question. Blackbeard crossed his arms triumphantly and sneered through thick tufts of dark facial hair.

"Lesson one: Why ya need a metaphysical regimen. Firstly, there's yer physical body, the material one ya left upstairs, consistin' of calcium, carbon, water, and so on. It's also known as 'dinner' if ya happen to be a worm."

The pirate smiled and scanned the small group of boys around him, as if expecting hearty laughter. But, judging by the grave faces staring back at him, the humor of the situation was lost upon them. He clapped his dusty hands together.

"Movin' right along, there's yer etheric body, the energetic shadow of yer physical body. That's what ya are now . . . etheric bodies. Without 'em, yer physical body just dissolves back into the elements from which it came."

This was a lot of information, even for Milton. He could tell by the concerned expressions of his classmates that they were still hung up on the worm part. Milton raised his hand.

"Yes, dear," Blackbeard said. "I mean, ya pathetic minnow."

"Um, right," replied Milton. "If this etheric body is so important, how come the scientists on the Surface haven't found it?"

Blackbeard tilted his head back and laughed until the gash in his neck opened wide. His mirth abruptly ceased, though its trail seeped out a bit from his exposed throat. He set his head straight and continued.

"Yer physical body is made up of trillions of wee atoms, but most of those atoms is nothin' but empty space . . . or at least that's what those pasty-faced, land-lubbing smarty-britches upstairs think! In those trillions o' teensy pockets is where yer etheric body lives, or lived, anyway. That's why ya still look like ya did, because yer arranged the same way, only it's just yer energy, not yer flesh suit."

A bucktoothed boy tentatively raised his hand.

"About the worms . . . ," he squeaked.

Exasperated, Blackbeard rolled his eyes.

"Aye, enough already of the worms . . . I'm sorry I

ever brought up the worms! The point is, yer still mostly who ya were. And while that's comfortin' and all, it doesn't mean ya can loaf belowdecks all day. Ya got to keep yer etheric body in shape, or else it'll stretch apart."

"Stretch?" Milton said.

"Looks like we've got a parrot in the audience!" Blackbeard bellowed heartily. "Wake up before I hang ya lot from the yardarm!!"

The boys looked fearfully around the gym for anything resembling either a yard or an arm.

"Yer all energy now, ya vermin. And energy can dissipate. And what happens when ya dissipate . . . ?"

Milton began to answer, but the pirate had meant the question rhetorically.

"Ya fade away, that's what ya do! So keep yerselves together, ya rottin' cackle fruits . . . lit'rally! Hence me trimmin' yer jibs 'bout a comprehensive metaphysical education routine!"

"So," a boy with feathered blond hair asked, "when our . . . *etheric* bodies came down here, that's why it hurt and stuff?"

"Good question, buccaneer." Blackbeard grinned. "If I had a piece of eight, I'd fling it at yer girly mop! That searin' tingle ya all felt was yer sentient body comin' apart."

How many bodies can one person have? thought Milton.

"Yer sentient body is the glue that keeps yer physical and etheric bodies hitched together tighter than a sailor's knot. When ya die, the energy's absorbed into the Transdimensional Power Grid as a kind o' tax to help cover the expense of sortin' ya lot out."

Milton raised his hand again.

"Yes, ya candidate for a keelhaul!"

"Right . . . yes . . . I felt a weird, I don't know, *feeling*. Like a bug being stared at through a big magnifying glass, only I was the bug, and the magnifying glass could see deep inside of me, in places I didn't even know I had. It happened right after my sentient body fell apart. I saw bright lights and clouds, even heard some pretty music. Then, all of a sudden, I came down here."

Blackbeard screwed up his already screwed-up face.

"That's a load of bilgewater, son," he replied in a breathy tone that caused the skin around his neck scar to wiggle. "Yer judged in an instant. Boom, done. No hitch about it. Certainly no heavenly glimpses as yer spinnin'. No knots on the rope o' judgment. Ya must be imaginin' things to ease yer guilt-logged conscience."

"No, sir," Milton replied. "I really . . ."

The pirate stormed off. Milton decided to keep his hatch closed about the weird conversation he heard in his head on the way down to Heck. He didn't need to give Blackbeard another reason to hang him from the yardarm.

"Follow me, ya worthless chests of fool's gold," Blackbeard said quickly.

The boys dragged themselves toward a crude wooden structure: basically two ladders—side by side—with long planks nailed to the top, with most of each plank jutting out like twin diving boards. Below the boards were deep buckets of what looked like chewing tobacco spit.

Blackbeard's chest swelled with pride.

"Welcome aboard *Queen Anne's Revenge*," he said with a grand sweep of his arm. "It's a partial model of the forty-gun warship I, um . . . *borrowed* . . . from a French privateer."

"Partial is right," Virgil whispered to Milton.

"Sorry," Blackbeard said, cupping his ear with his hand, "did ya say that ya wanna go first? Well, shiver me timbers, come on up, yer the next contestant on Walk the Plank!"

Virgil shuffled forward glumly to a chorus of wicked laughter.

"And don't ferget yer parrot, ya tub o' blubber!"

Milton sighed and joined his friend as he marched toward the planks. Virgil and Milton climbed their respective ladders.

"Now, crew," Blackbeard continued, "walkin' the plank is that rarest of exercises: one that is both toning and fun to watch! It helps tighten the etheric muscle shadows on yer legs and stern, and helps yer sense of balance, which is no pleasure cruise when yer body is cracklin' with restless energy!"

Virgil and Milton stood atop their ladders, Virgil's creaking under the strain.

"Step lively, lads. Up to the edge, now. Good, good."

Milton toed the wooden precipice and looked down into the frothy brown maw of the bucket below.

"Now, ya bloated carcasses, hop up and down on the plank and wave yer arms like a mother gull protectin' her squabs."

Milton hopped and waved his arms, but under protest.

"Why do we have to wave our arms?" Milton asked, desperately attempting to maintain his balance.

"Why ya ask, Cap'n Question Mark? Well . . . mainly because it's a right good laugh!"

The class exploded in contemptuous laughter. Virgil's platform shook and wobbled as if under siege by an invisible storm.

"Now, I want ya to jump yerselves in the briny brink on the count o' three . . ."

Milton gagged.

"One . . . two . . ."

The class bell tolled. Blackbeard's face drooped down to his billowing once-white shirt.

Milton and Virgil stopped jumping and smiled at each other with relief.

"Aye, well I'll be measured for me chains. Ya all have permission to go ashore . . ."

As Virgil tried to maneuver himself back down his ladder, he lost his balance. The rickety platform, with its twin planks and ladders, wobbled past the point of no return. The wooden structure toppled to the ground, knocking over the enormous buckets of lumpy, tarlike drool.

Milton and Virgil lay paralyzed in the warm, expanding puddle.

Their classmates got one last laugh before heading out into the hallway for the cafeterium and their afternoon snack.

Blackbeard stood over the miserable boys, who twitched in the pool of backwash.

"Well, blow me down!" he snickered. "Looks like the fates have run a rig on ya two!"

He did a merry little jig toward a closet in the corner, emerging with two mops and buckets. He skipped back, whistling, and then dropped the bundle in front of the two boys, still stunned on their backs.

"Once you've swabbed this sick off of me floor, then ya two can . . . *swab the deck*!"

The pirate's eyes glittered with delight. Milton rose cautiously, hoping to avoid contact with the remains of Blackbeard's tobacco binge as much as possible.

"What deck?" Milton asked.

Blackbeard's expression sagged like a sail in a sudden

calm. "Er, I mean . . ." He straightened and coughed. "Ya two can swab the hallway. And swab it good! No lollygagging or hornswoggling, either! I want a floor as bright as the sunrise over the Caribbean, aye?"

"Yes, sir," Virgil mumbled as he stood up, then quivered and quaked before slipping back down into the revolting spew.

Blackbeard stepped out for a nip of Nelson's Folly, whatever that was. Milton just hoped it wasn't a brand of chewing tobacco.

As Milton and Virgil finally emerged from the sludge, Virgil picked up a mop and, like a natural born deckhand, began swabbing.

"And to think," he muttered, "I used to love playing pirates."

The two boys swabbed in silence, until Virgil began to hum a familiar tune, occasionally breaking into song. "Up, up and away, my beautiful, my beautiful balloon . . ."

The desperately cheery music haunted Milton's thoughts. *A balloon . . . floating . . . up, up and away.*

Treat this whole thing like an algebra problem, Milton reflected. $X + y + z = escape.$ *A balloon. But how? What were x, y, and z?*

Then, after all of the variables wrestled with one another in Milton's mind, he began to see a pattern. A chain of small events, arranged just so, floated to the top of his thoughts. If executed properly—and in the correct sequence—these variables, events, whatever, could lead to something . . . *big*. The details needed to be worked out, but Milton knew that he not only had an answer, he had *the* answer.

Milton grinned uncontrollably. His heart was filled with music.

Up, up and away, my beautiful, my beautiful balloon . . .

30 · TOUCHED BY AN ANGEL

JUST WHEN SHE thought she understood Heck, something happened to make Marlo thoroughly lose her psychic balance.

"Well, I've got a hammer . . ."

Here she was in a white floor-length robe with ten other girls on a riser singing while an angel waved her baton in time with the music.

". . . All over this land"

The angel, Ms. Von Trapp, grinned and clapped her creased, delicate hands together.

"Vunderbar! Vunderbar!" She beamed with a gleeful flap of her wings.

"Did she just say Wonderbra?" Lyon snickered to Bordeaux, who were both in the back row, totally *not* singing. Lyon noticed Marlo looking over at them.

"Yeah," replied Bordeaux, "and it's a wonder if Gotharella over there will ever *need* a bra!"

Marlo's face flushed. She had dealt with Lyon and Bordeaux's type before, on the Surface. Popular, cruel . . . Usually it was just a case of trading barbs before merging back into the shadows. But, down here, she was off her game.

Ms. Von Trapp glided across the floor to the riser. "Zat vas very good!" she said. "The flavors of your voices are blending beautifully, like crisp apple strudel! Now let us try something more fundamental . . . heavy on zee fun!"

The girls groaned as Ms. Von Trapp tuned her guitar and struggled to get the strap over her left wing.

"Here ve go, girls. Very simple."

She cleared her throat and out came a voice as clear and pure as a lake of holy water.

"Do-re-mi-fa-so-la-ti-do."

The girls grudgingly joined voices. Marlo sang quietly to herself, though perhaps "sing" is overstating it a bit. Sounds came out of her mouth, but they were more like gnarled tangles of sonic barbed wire than melodies.

A pasty girl with jagged chunks cut off of her dark hair stopped singing.

"Hey," the girl said groggily, stretching the word "hey" out until it was two syllables. "This is, like, that song from the movie. The movie with all the singing and Nazis, where the hills are alive."

The other girls nodded to one another.

"Yeah," said a squat girl with mangled orthodontia. "Doe, a deer . . ."

Half the girls were now singing ". . . a female deer . . ."

A small cloud drifted across Ms. Von Trapp's sunny disposition.

"Now, girls, let us . . ."

"Ray, a drop . . ."

"Please . . ."

". . . of golden sun . . ."

"QUIET, OR YOU'LL GET ZHA BUSINESS END OF MY BATON!"

The song was snuffed out like a candle. The girls were petrified.

Ms. Von Trapp was trembling, strangling the neck of her guitar. A lone white feather zigzagged down from her wings. She noted its passage with shame. The wrinkled angel closed her eyes and clasped her hands together in prayer. After a moment of perfect stillness, she wiped a gleaming tear from her cheek and composed herself.

"Girls . . . *young ladies* . . . ," she said contritely. "*Entschuldigung.* I must apologize for my outburst. I'm not used to being down here."

She smoothed her immaculate robes.

"Perhaps ve take a break from zee singing. Do you *schön Mädchens* have any questions?"

Lyon raised her hand. "Yes," she said tartly, "I don't know who Sean Munchkin is, but I have a question: what is an angel doing here, anyway?"

Murmurs rippled through the choir of dead young women. The angel's smile shone like a miniature sun. The girls collectively winced at its brilliance.

"It's Title VII of zha Eternal Quality Unification Adherence Law, better known as EQUAL," Ms. Von Trapp said. "It means zat representatives from various otherworldly dominions are allowed to enter other realms as missionaries, to ensure that every soul has a truly balanced supernatural education."

Bordeaux's already slack, lip-glossed mouth gaped wider.

"So, like, you're here to, um . . . show us how good it is to be good or something?"

Ms. Von Trapp smiled affectionately. "Something like zhat, my little frau."

Lyon put her hands where her hips should have been.

"You're wasting your time," she said with a sharp voice like a slap. "Being bad is fun. So pack up your stupid guitar, Sister Act, and fly back up to your boring old cloud."

Throughout Lyon's tirade, Ms. Von Trapp just grinned compassionately.

"*Danke* for your opinion, Miss Sheraton," the angel replied with a glimmer of pity in her eyes. "It is true, I may indeed be vasting my time . . ."

The skin around her eyes crinkled as her smile spread wider across her face. *Did she have surgery to shorten her cheek muscles?* Marlo pondered.

". . . but I have all zha time in zha world . . . and then some."

Lyon looked at Bordeaux confused and subtly deflated.

"In any case," Ms. Von Trapp continued while returning to her place behind the plywood lectern, "it is a nonissue as I have been . . . reassigned."

Figures, Marlo thought. Whenever she encountered a halfway-decent teacher, they either ended up getting transferred, fired, or, in her ex-hippie art teacher's case, quitting to tour with a rock band as their interpretive dancer.

"Now, before ve end our class," Ms. Von Trapp said with a lump in her devout throat, "I vould like to teach you a little song that you might find useful ven facing some of the more . . . *impressionable* demons down here."

The Austrian angel cleared her throat.

"Kum ba yah, my Lord, kum ba yah!
Kum ba yah, my Lord, kum ba yah!
Kum ba yah, my Lord, kum ba yah!
O Lord, kum ba yah!"

Slowly the girls—save gifted mouthers Lyon and Bordeaux—joined in. Marlo found the song oddly comforting, despite the fact that she either missed or fatally wounded every note.

The class bell tolled, and the girls filed off the riser to hang their robes on rusty hooks. Lyon and Bordeaux dropped their robes on the floor, assuming some faceless person would pick them up for them, as they always did.

"Auf wiedersehen, children," the angel said sweetly as the girls shuffled past her. "Remember: you cry a little and zen you wait for the sun to come out. It always does."

"Ooh," Lyon mocked, "and I forgot to pack my sunscreen before I died."

Lyon and Bordeaux cackled as they entered the hallway. Marlo straggled behind, her head down so that no one would see her blotchy, tear-streaked face. That's all she needed, she fumed: to have Lyon and Bordeaux see her in a moment of weakness.

Just outside the classroom, gently ruffling in front of her awful Birkenstocks, was a long, perfectly white feather. The sight of it filled Marlo with quiet cheer.

She picked it up and rushed back to Ms. Von Trapp's classroom.

"Here," she said as she burst through the door, "I thought you might want . . ."

But the room was empty. The only movement came from swirling dust motes that slowly settled to the ground.

There was an overpowering smell in the room: sweet, sour, and comforting. Like rose water, cedar, mothballs, and soap. It smelled like her Grandma Fauster. It was a smell she used to make fun of. But now, it made her feel safe and hopeful. It was the smell of an angel.

Marlo set the feather on the lectern and left the classroom. She sulked down the smoky hallway on her way to the cafeterium. Suddenly it dawned on her: she had found something and *not* pocketed it. And an angel's feather at that. What a score! But the thought of keeping it hadn't even occurred to her. What was happening to her? Being dead she could deal with, but not knowing who she was anymore, that was something else.

31 · LIVER LET DIE

MILTON SNEAKED INTO the empty cafeterium and leaned his mop against an Automat machine. He had never had any strong feelings regarding mops before. But after spending what felt like hours swabbing—yet was probably "no time at all" in this irritating place—he had developed a strong animosity toward this otherwise useful cleaning tool.

Luckily for Milton, Blackbeard had "hit the head," whatever that was. He was just glad that, if a head was to be hit, it wasn't going to be his.

He plucked a scrap of paper from the bulletin board. The flyer had a pathetic picture of a sad little Latin boy from Snivel on it pleading for a pen pal. Someone had drawn a mustache and horns on him and written "Cry Baby" across his face. Milton flipped the piece of paper over and dug into his backpack for a pencil.

"Oww!!" Milton yelped. He sucked his bleeding finger. Cerberus, disguised as Lucky, popped his head out of Milton's bag and spat out a wicked hiss, fresh blood staining his muzzle red.

"What's the deal?" Milton sniffed. "You've never done that before . . . You must be hungry."

Lucky strained to escape the tightly secured knapsack.

"Don't be a fuzzy little fool," Milton scolded. "The way you've been acting lately, you'd just get caught and fed to that ugly, three-headed dog."

Lucky growled viciously at Milton. His contact lens cameras flared red like a hot spark before fading back into the creature's angry stare.

"I'll get you something to eat in just a second," Milton soothed while trying to quell an uneasiness he'd never had before with his usually faithful pet.

Milton cased out the cafeterium nervously. It was empty. He took the pencil and scrawled a quick message to Marlo.

He felt good about Operation Up, Up and Away (every mission needed a cool name, Milton thought). Marlo's escape plan that she had hatched when they first arrived had suffered from the fact that it had never, at any point, been *planned.* It was just an act of spontaneous bravado. What it had in spunk and daring, it lacked in foresight and follow-through. Virgil's attempt at freedom actually had a shape. Yet, like its architect, that shape was large, soft, and impossible to wrap your arms around. It depended too much on faith: faith in the map, faith in circumstance, faith in everything just magically falling into place.

Milton still didn't know what to expect if he did break out of Heck, free from Principal Bubb's claws. But it almost didn't matter. The plan itself—specifically the process of solving a problem—gave Milton a purpose. It was the only thing holding him together.

He didn't have the time—or the space—to go into great detail about the plan in his note, just the specifics important to Marlo: to be prepared tonight, to meet in the cafeterium after the big midnight flush, and that he and Marlo would both storm the Assessment Chamber to grab as many jars of buoyant, blobby lost souls as they could hold.

Milton finished his note and opened the compartment containing the undisturbed slab of liver. The fake ferret wriggled through a breach in the knapsack's flap to better smell the rancid meat. The creature's wild eyes again flared red as glowing coals.

Bea "Elsa" Bubb's surveillance pod rumbled in her sealskin fanny pack. She rubbed her swollen abdomen.

"Darn spotted owl enchilada," she grumbled. "You never eat it so much as rent it."

The pod buzzed again, and the digestively distressed principal finally located the rumble's source.

She fished it out of her pack and flicked it on.

Grainy images flashed across the tiny screen. Cerberus was obviously agitated and the screen was often a trembling blur. But she could make out two key images: one, the words "Marlo" and "escape" written on a note, and two, the slick lump of dark brown meat the note was slid under.

"Liver," Principal Bubb muttered angrily. *"Liver note."* She jabbed the device crossly with her thumb to turn it off.

The principal rose, kicked off her taxidermied bunny slippers, and stepped toward the door. She stopped, however, in mid-stride, and looked down at Lucky—the *real* Lucky—twitching irritably in his cage.

"I'm stepping out for a bite to eat, you musky little monster," she taunted. "Can I get you anything? Perhaps a nice, juicy rodent? Or a heaping bowl of Weasel Chow?"

To a ferret, time is defined as the spaces between meals and naps. Trapped in this tiny cage in this stinky room with the loud, stinky lady, Lucky hadn't had either since . . . since the last time he had eaten or slept. The point is that it felt like a really long time.

"Cat got your tongue?" the principal teased. "Oh, how I wish. Well, you look like you could use some slimming down anyhow. I have your best interests at heart, you adorable little coat-to-be. So no matter how much you beg, I promise not to break down and feed you."

She opened the door and trod out into the hallway. *"Ciao!"* Bea "Elsa" Bubb chirped with a blithe wave of her claw before slamming the door behind her.

Lucky circled the cage frantically, as if spiraling down an invisible drain. He pressed his head between the bars of his cage, but—again—only got as far as his belly. He was closer this time, though. He could just puke up the paper he had eaten, but the boy thought it very important, and he must bring it back to him, no matter what. So he kept circling and circling and circling well past the point of exhaustion. Just another ounce to go, and he would be free . . . or be the smelly old bag's new ferret stole.

32 · GIRLS AND PLOYS

Want to make lots of money and earn swell prizes, too: like this
BRIGHT RED SPORTS CAR*? Of course you do! Sell **GYP**,
Heck's crispest newspaper! In your spare time! Every week!
FOREVER AND EVER! Make ten, sometimes twenty Cana-
dian cents a week! We want to get you started on a profitable
business of your own! **REALLY! NO FOOLIN'!**™ As soon as
your signature is dry on the handy coupon below, you'll get
stacks and stacks of **GYP** immediately! And you pay only for
the copies you don't sell! That sounds fair, doesn't it? Of
course it does! Sign **NOW, NOW, NOW!**

*You will never, ever get a bright red sports car.

"NO, NO, NO . . . ," Marlo muttered. She ripped the ad off
of the cafeterium bulletin board.

Marlo walked over toward the Automat machines,

passing Lyon, Bordeaux, and various snobby bleached-blond preadolescent acolytes.

"It's probably a good idea to explore other career options," Lyon snickered, referring to the ad in Marlo's hand. "You certainly wouldn't cut it as a singer! Your voice could raise the dead!"

The scary-thin girls cackled sharply.

"*I wish,*" Marlo said while walking past them.

She stopped in her tracks, her ugly Birkenstocks squeaking to a halt. Bea "Elsa" Bubb was loitering by the Automat machines—looking anxious and out of place—peering into the doors. She never ate here, or at least Marlo hadn't seen her during the last two . . . *whatevers* . . . here in Limbo. She also noticed that Principal Bubb was trying really hard *not* to look at Marlo with those creepy, lizard-like eyes of hers. And, of course, her trying not to look like she was looking at her meant that she really *was* looking at her, peripherally. (Didn't Milton once say that lizards were good at seeing sideways? Now she wished that she had paid attention to her little brother once in a while.)

Fortunately, Marlo had already read Milton's note, which she promptly ate. It was probably the tastiest thing down here anyhow.

The principal laid her sick yellow-green eyes on the liver, then leaned against the foul food machine, whistling nonchalantly.

She totally *knows,* Marlo thought.

Marlo sat down at a nearby table and dashed out her note. Only this wasn't the note she had intended to write, basically telling Milton that he had a decent idea for once and that she'd meet him later tonight as planned. Instead she wrote the following:

MILTON (FAUSTER, LITTLE GUY WITH GLASSES),
   I, MARLO (FAUSTER, YOUR SISTER, EXOTIC BEAUTY WITH UNIQUE FASHION SENSE), WILL MOST DEFINITELY ESCAPE WITH YOU THE DAY AFTER TOMORROW. YOUR PLAN TO AGAIN GO DOWN THE RIVER STYX IS BRILLIANT. SO, ONCE MORE WITH FEELING, SEE YOU THE DAY AFTER TOMORROW.
   I LOOK FORWARD TO OUR ESCAPE DOWN THE RIVER STYX.

                         YOURS IN FREEDOM,
                         MARLO (FAUSTER)

She smiled to herself. *Brilliant*, Marlo reflected with pride. *This way anything we do that's suspicious will just be expected, only Bubba will be at the wrong place at the wrong time.*

Marlo pretended to slyly sidle over to the Automat machines, where she openly surveyed the liver, slipped the note underneath, then put it back in its compartment and closed the door.

Trap baited. Marlo smirked.

She walked past Lyon and her pride, who were simply licking their food and putting it back on their plates to avoid contact with calories.

"Bonjour, ladies." Marlo smiled as she sashayed out the door. "I really must be going."

Lyon and Bordeaux gaped at each other. Lyon sneered with indignation that Marlo actually had the gall to address her.

"Whatever, abra*cadaver,*" she called out, much to the malicious delight of her fellow food lickers.

Bea "Elsa" Bubb opened the liver compartment and pulled out the putrid gland and accompanying note. Her serpent eyes narrowed and darkened to red. She crumpled up the note in her shaking fist.

"So I was right," she seethed. "Escape the day after tomorrow? Not on my shift, sister."

She shoved the spoiled liver lump into her mouth and chewed it savagely.

"You mess with a demon, you get the horns."

33 · SWEET DREAMS
AREN'T MADE OF THIS

THE HARSH FLUORESCENT lights outside of the Boys' Totally Bunks flashed on and off.

You have to give credit to Blackbeard, Milton thought between each painful step as he dragged himself toward the bunks. *He really knows how to give one heck of a metaphysical workout.*

Bea "Elsa" Bubb seemed to emerge from a puff of smoke in the entryway, waving a screeching, ear-splitting bullhorn.

"Lights-out, ladies," she snorted. "You have a big day tomorrow. You'll need to get your beauty sleep."

Inside the filthy bunker, miserable boys were lined up by pitschspork-prodding demons to put on woven-hair pajamas.

"What's tomorrow?" Milton whispered to Virgil as he stepped into his scratchy nightclothes.

"It's the first day of the rest of your afterlife, when you find out which circle of Heck you'll be assigned to," hissed Bea "Elsa" Bubb, who was suddenly, inexplicably, by Milton's side. Milton fell over, his pajama bottoms around his ankles, in shock. The other boys laughed to take their minds off the itching.

"I wouldn't want you to miss a single, gruesome detail," she said with breath like rotten fish, holding out her claw to help him up. Milton stared at her extended claw and righted himself with clumsy effort.

Damian strutted into the barracks like royalty.

"I'm *baaaaaack*," he said while undoing his gold HADES cuff links. "Did you miss me?"

Bea "Elsa" Bubb walked up to Damian and gave him a little pinch on the cheek, then turned to inspect the group of gawking boys.

"Now get in your pajamas, boys, or I'll be forced to read you some of my poetry."

The crowd of boys collectively gasped and cleared away from the principal as if she had the plague—which was ridiculous; she had gotten over that years ago.

The throng of boys padded down the dank aisles of the barracks. Principal Bubb herded the boys past a dusty table set with pitchers brimming with murky water.

"Now, boys," she chirped. "Be sure to drink your special water. It'll help you sleep."

She snapped her talons and suddenly the boys were clutching their throats with extreme thirst. They slogged down the foul water, as little rivers trickled down their necks.

Milton put down his pitcher and belched, throwing up just a bit. (Corn? He hadn't eaten corn in weeks . . .) He walked over to a bunk with his name etched on it. Damian shoved him harshly aside.

"Oh, joy. We're bunkmates," the hulking bully said, staring at his name below Milton's. "I'll give you two seconds to climb out of my sight, or else I'll blow you up again."

Milton crawled up the rotten rope ladder, which wriggled and swayed in his labored attempt to scale it.

As soon as Milton laid his head on the pillow, serpents slithered from either side of his body, coiling together in the middle to tie themselves into knots, until Milton was bound tight to the bed. The room was filled with the noise of struggling boys.

Bea "Elsa" Bubb stopped short in the doorway on her way out. She cast a giant frightening shadow across the rows of squirming boys.

"I hear Sadia's very nice this time of year, Mr. Fauster," she said sweetly. "All the boys have such lovely bruises . . ."

34 · IF YOU SNOOZE, YOU LOSE

MILTON FOUGHT TO stay awake. He did fierce mental battle with a creeping fatigue. Swabbing had mercilessly worked muscles Milton didn't even know he had.

But resist the velvety fog of sleep he must if he was going to break out of this place, this boil on the butt of the hereafter. So Milton filled his head with exciting things, such as his favorite passage from *Moby-Dick*:

> *Yonder, by the ever-brimming goblet's rim, the warm waves blush like wine. The diver sun goes down; my soul mounts up! She wearies with her endless hill. Is, then, the crown too heavy that I wear? The crown that coils around my head like a ferret, covered with Christmas tinsel, before bursting open with savage demon claws . . .*

Milton jolted awake with a start. The ol' white whale—which clearly represents the power that limits and controls man—was evidently not up to the task. Instead, Milton filled his mind with thrilling math problems.

A box contains thirty red balls and fifty blue balls. Six balls are randomly selected from the box without replacement. What is the probability of selecting a red ball followed by a blue ball, then a red ball followed by a blue ball, then a red ball followed by a blue ball? Round your answer to the nearest thousandth.

Hmm . . . let's see, Milton thought. *If the red ball, followed by the blue . . . wait . . . how can I count all these when someone is shaking the box . . . shaking it . . . shaking . . .*

"Milton!" Virgil hissed while shaking his friend awake.

Milton, again, was abruptly roused from a sleep he didn't know he was sleeping. Beneath him, the malevolent bulk that was Damian shifted restlessly in his bunk.

"It's time," Virgil murmured. "It's now or never."

Milton nodded, put on his bent, fractured glasses, and then struggled to free himself from his serpent restraints. He tried getting skinny (a trick he learned from Lucky) . . . Close but no chocolate cigar.

"Here," Virgil said. "I got something that might help."

He reached inside his scratchy pajamas and pulled out a small Styrofoam cup of castor oil. Milton arched his eyebrow at his husky friend.

"You know, in case I got thirsty in the middle of the night," Virgil replied.

He poured the fishy goop on and around Milton's unyielding serpents. Virgil poked his pudgy fingers beneath the snakes to better distribute the oil while Milton wriggled. Finally, Milton slithered out of his bunk and onto the cold, marble floor.

As Milton tried desperately to rub off the thick, briny oil, he eyed his friend.

"How did *you* get out?"

Virgil looked down, his round jowly cheeks flushing red.

"Um," he whispered, "my snakes were so exhausted from wrapping around me all night, they just . . . gave up."

Milton smiled. "See, there *are* advantages to having an eating disorder coupled with a thyroid condition!"

Virgil grinned back. Just then there was a sizzling hiss from Milton's knapsack. Milton grabbed his bag off of the bed and clutched it close.

"Quiet, Lucky," he scolded into the bag, then stared at Damian's unconscious form for any sign of rousing. "What are you trying to do, get us caught?"

The faux ferret glared back at Milton. Its eyes glowed wickedly in the dark. If glares were a language, this particular one would mean "Yes, I am indeed trying to get you caught."

"Geez," mumbled Milton as he strapped the bag to

his back. "Whatever's got into him, I wish it would get out. Let's scram before Sleeping Bully wakes up."

Milton and Virgil tiptoed across the Boys' Totally Bunks floor. They gently nudged open the door, which creaked like an arthritic dinosaur. Inside Milton's knapsack, "Lucky" was hopping mad, hopping madly.

They sidled against the hallways as stealthily as two boys in hair pajamas possibly could. They were hoping to flee through the cafeterium and break into the Disorientation Center. Unfortunately, two hall demonitors were chatting it up in the hallway between the boys' classrooms and the cafeterium.

"Okay," whispered Virgil, "you're not going to like this, but it looks like we're going to have to resort to Plan B."

Milton vibrated with a full-body shudder. "I don't know what's worse," he murmured, "eternal torment or . . . Plan B."

35 · DREAM SCHEME

MARLO TROD SOFTLY down the hallway and peered around the corner. Yep, she hadn't been hearing voices. Just outside the cafeterium several hall demonitors chatted casually to each other about the sorry state of their secondhand pitchsporks.

Hmm, Marlo mused. *Looks like Plan B . . . whatever that is.*

But Marlo was always one for improvising. Any criminal artist worth her salt was most inspired when straying beyond the safety of a fully baked plan. Perhaps that was why most of the truly great ones were currently serving time.

She stole back to her bunk with an idea Easy-Baking in her head. Marlo's serpent restraints were still smarting from her pointy fangs—which had given them both matching hickeys—and recoiled upon her return.

Marlo fluffed up her unfluffable pillow and pretended to be asleep. After a few minutes of snoring to create the appropriate mood, she began to laugh uproariously. She plastered the front of her head with the goofiest, most blissed-out grin imaginable and thrashed about in an approximation of total, unconscious ecstasy.

Lyon stirred and slipped off her blindfold.

"Put a cork in it, thrift store," she yapped. "Someone as beautiful as me needs lots of sleep!"

Within seconds the hall demonitors stormed into the Girls' Totally Bunks.

"What's not wrong?" a slimy white demon that resembled a huge maggot with a goat's head inquired. "We heard the most terrible sound."

"It's that loopy loser over there," Lyon said with a wag of her long, perfectly manicured finger. "She's acting like there's a nitrous leak in her head."

The demon guards exchanged sober glances. A spindly, praying mantis–ish demon gulped hard.

"Sounds like . . ."

The three of them looked toward Marlo, who was beaming from ear to ear in utter delight.

". . . a happy dream!"

The three demons rushed Marlo into the Girls' Unrestrooms.

"Quick," said the goat maggot, "get her in the shower."

They shoved her into a grimy stall and turned on

the cold, runny mud. It was all Marlo could do to stay in character.

"It's no use," said a squat, standard-issue, inside-out meat demon. "She's still dreaming and . . . *smiling.*"

The demons were deeply disturbed as they cradled the unconscious, grinning girl under the lumpy stream of mud.

Just then Principal Bubb burst into the Unrestrooms. She was wearing an immodest marshmallow Peeps–skin robe and her hair was in curlers. Unfortunately that hair was on her back.

"I got here as fast as I could," Principal Bubb snarled. "Would one of you three stooges tell me what is going on?"

The goat-maggot demoness stepped forward.

"It seems like she is having a dream," she said.

"And?" asked Principal Bubb unimpressed.

The demon looked at its hooves. "And it's, apparently, a really happy one."

The Principal of Darkness gasped.

"It can't be," she muttered in disbelief. "This whole facility is shielded with good-dream-resistant paint. This must be some kind of trick."

She leaned close to Marlo.

"Of course," Bea "Elsa" Bubb said, sneering, "the Fauster girl."

Marlo had to bite her tongue hard to keep from trembling and focus on her cheerful charade.

"Miss Fauster," Principal Bubb demanded sternly. "Are you having a . . . nice dream? If this is some kind of deception, I guarantee that . . ."

"Unicorns," Marlo mumbled with a dopey smile.

"What did she say?" Bea "Elsa" Bubb asked the head hall demonitor.

"It sounded like she said—"

"And butterflies," Marlo continued dreamily. "Laughing happy butterflies fluttering over a field of daffodils, swaying in a sweet, fragrant breeze."

Principal Bubb staggered back in horror.

"This is worse than I thought! Get her to the nurse's office at once before her condition spreads!"

As the demons rushed out, Principal Bubb clutched her lower abdomen.

"Cursed irritable bowel syndrome," she moaned as she raced toward a stall. "These wretched children are wreaking havoc on my intestinal tract."

Moments later Marlo was on a gurney carried by her dutiful demons through KinderScare to the infirmary. Marlo turned on her side, still smiling though the muscles in her face were aching, and spied the shaking little boy undergoing phonics cold turkey. Marlo winked at the boy and mouthed several challenging vowel combinations. The boy's eyes glazed over and a knowing smile crossed his face.

36 · MOON RIVER

"MAYBE WE CAN just wait the demons out," Milton stalled. "They can't talk forever . . . well, sure, they can talk forever, because they're undead and this is Limbo, but I seriously doubt that, since they basically share the same experiences day in and day out, not that there are days here really, but at some point, sooner or later, they'll *have* to run out of things to—"

Virgil slapped Milton across the face. Milton stared blankly at his friend.

"Get a grip," Virgil said calmly. "We've got to keep it together. Those demons there change everything. Now the only way to get to the Assessment Chamber, Mr. Dior's office, and to the gates is Plan B—back down into the sewer, crawling beneath the guards."

Milton rubbed his stinging cheek. "Get a grip? I'm

not the one who's hitting people for no reason. *Fine.* Plan B. Sure. Bring it on."

Milton and Virgil slunk quietly away toward the Unrestrooms.

Unfortunately, unbeknowst to them, the trio of hall demonitors left their posts only moments later, racing toward the Girls' Totally Bunks. As the two boys made their way down the hallway, they heard voices drifting from the faculty barracks, mainly drunken "arghs" and "yo-ho-hos." Milton's swabbing muscles ached at the sound of Blackbeard's voice, like a dog conditioned to drool at the sound of a bell.

"By the sound of his yo-ho-ho, it seems as though Blackbeard has found himself a bottle of rum," Virgil commented under his labored breath.

Milton didn't say a word, partly to remain unde-tected (and avoid any midnight swabbing) and partly because he was still mad at Virgil. Sure, Milton was calmer now, but, boy, did his cheek sting.

They slinked into the Boys' Unrestrooms and went to the dreaded stall.

Virgil looked over at his trembling friend.

"We're becoming pros at this." He grinned. "And this time, even though we're not growing any older, we have to be growing at least a little wiser, huh?"

Milton smiled despite himself. He breathed in his last lungful of not-completely-gross air, squeezed his eyes shut, and—for the second time in two days—plunged into the most disgusting place imaginable.

He crawled through the slimy pipeline on his hands and knees. It was extra slick due to a fresh batch of sewage from the Surface. Judging from its sickening warmth and suffocating stench, it couldn't be more than a few hours old.

Just as Milton managed to crawl around a particularly nasty clot of waste, he was flipped over by a great wave of filth from behind. Virgil had collapsed into a pool of putrid poop with a massive belly flop. Milton emerged from the murk, coated like the Creature from the Brown Lagoon. All that was recognizably Milton was the icy glare from beyond his grimy glasses.

"Sorry," Virgil bleated sheepishly. "I'm not exactly the most graceful diver."

Milton shivered uncontrollably. "C'mon," he said through chattering teeth. "We've got to tell Marlo we're knee-deep in Plan B."

Down the main pipe, many yards away, they could see shiny new sheets of metal grating blocking passage for larger "waste."

"Seems like they'll be no more trips to Purgatory any time soon," Virgil said.

"Fine by me," Milton grumbled.

They inched their way around several sharp turns until, after forty fecal feet or so, they arrived just below the Girls' Unrestrooms. Milton looked up toward the sole pipe that led to the girls' bathroom. *Dozens and dozens of dead girls vying for one dirty toilet must be a particularly* feminine *form of punishment,* he thought.

"Okay, I'll be right back," Milton croaked, "boldly going where no man has gone before." Virgil touched knuckles with Milton.

"Be brave, bro. And don't worry: what happens in Heck, *stays* in Heck."

Milton nodded and with a steely look of determination scaled the poopy pipe to rouse his sister before she stumbled into a demons' nest.

He worked his way up through the cramped tube until he saw, just a few yards above him, a faint light illuminating the glistening gunk. Milton elbowed his way upward until his head was just flush with the rim of the toilet. Then, like a sudden eclipse, the dim glow was obscured by a great, terrible something—three moons, by the looks of it. Only these unheavenly objects were not moons (well, not in the astronomical sense). They belonged to none other than Principal Bubb. And they were getting closer. Milton had a rim-side seat to the dark side of her moons, which were setting quickly on him.

He dropped back down as fast as he could in a desperate attempt to avoid his principal expelling something terrible upon him.

He plopped beside Virgil in a soiled, agitated heap.

"Quick, Plan C!" Milton panted.

"Plan C?" questioned Virgil. "I don't think we made it that far down the alphabet."

"We've got to get out of the line of fire . . . Principal Bubb . . ."

"She's here?"

"Yeah, at twelve o'clock."

"You don't mean . . . ," Virgil said as the blood drained out of his face.

Milton and Virgil crawled away as fast as possible, while sickening splatters and putrid plops fell just behind them.

After scurrying only several dozen yet terribly crucial yards, the duo paused for a few fetid breaths.

"That was close," huffed Virgil.

"You have no idea," said Milton, trembling. "She must have been on a late-night sweep of the Girls' Totally Bunks and had to take a . . ."—Milton took a moment to dry-heave—". . . *potty* break."

"Hopefully she's not on her way to tuck us in, or we're toast."

Milton glared at Virgil.

"Whoops," Virgil replied contritely. "Sorry about that."

He rummaged through the pockets of his pajamas and pulled out the map.

"Why do you still carry that piece of junk with you?" Milton asked skeptically. "I mean, the *Secret Toilet*? C'mon. That map's about as accurate as a TV weatherman."

"Yeah," Virgil meekly acknowledged. "But it's all we've got."

"I guess," Milton replied with a shrug. "And some of it was right. Let me have a look."

Milton scrunched his eyes at the blotchy map.

"We were *here,*" Milton said, pointing at the Girls' Unrestrooms. "So it seems that, if we followed this pipe here," he continued, highlighting a tract of plumbing with a finger swipe, "it should lead us to . . ."

Milton gulped. Virgil leaned into the map.

"The 'facilities' in the teachers' lounge," Virgil concluded. "The closest bathroom to the gates."

"It's worth a try," Milton said, resigned. "I just hope we don't accidentally find ourselves in the colon of the thirty-seventh president of the United States."

37 · BOOGEY BOGEY

LIMBO, MILTON REALIZED, seemed a lot smaller when explored from below. In fact, after shuffling just several hundred filthy feet in the muck, Virgil stopped, looked down at the soiled map, then pointed to the roof of the tunnel a few yards in front of him.

"Here we are," he said. "Up, up and away . . ."

In my beautiful balloon, thought Milton hopefully.

Virgil squeezed through the potty pit. "All clear," he whispered back to Milton. Luckily for subterranean sewage travelers, the lavatory design down here was ample due to the varied demonic body types and, um, *volume* moved daily.

"They've actually got towels here," Virgil murmured as he flopped onto the marble floor. "And magazines less than a hundred years old."

Milton rose through the pit while Virgil caressed a roll of toilet paper.

"Wow, it's actual tissue," Virgil said with awe. "Cotton, by the feel of it. Not like that sandpaper they give us . . ."

"Shh," Milton hushed. "I hear something."

Milton and Virgil pressed open a heavy oak door, which seemed fashioned from the lid of a casket, and peered inside.

With his head on a table, Richard M. Nixon snored away, each horselike exhalation rippling his ash gray jowls.

"Yep, the teachers' lounge," Milton muttered. "Not quite the Secret Toilet outside the gates or whatever, but it's got to be closer than where we were at least. C'mon."

Milton and Virgil crept across the teachers' filthy kitchenette toward the door as Mr. Nixon muttered in his sleep.

"Watergate, Shmatergate . . . quit worrying, Spiro . . . there's no way we can get caught . . . no way . . . *no* . . ."

Milton opened the door gently and peeked into the foul playground. Empty, except for an electric toy bunny banging a tiny drum whose batteries were slowly dying.

"The coast is clear," Milton whispered. "You hide out in the broken bungle gym while I see if I can find Marlo . . . I just hope she had the good sense to . . ."

Milton twitched.

"*Good sense* . . . Oh, man . . ."

He turned to Virgil.

"If I'm not back in five minutes, go on without me."

Milton tiptoed through the foul playground, adopting a variety of stealth moves picked up from action movies, until he arrived at a shabby clubfoot house near the KinderScare facility. Between him and the Disorientation Center was a whole lot of nothing: just a big empty play area with nothing to hide behind. But he had to make a break for it.

"One . . . two . . . *three* . . . ," Milton said through clenched teeth. He lurched forward and sprinted across the concrete floor toward the Disorientation Center. Halfway there a large shaggy shape emerged from Kinder-Scare. A Boogeyperson on an interception course. Milton panicked, desperately gauging the creature's approximate speed in relationship to his and the distance he still had to run.

As the creature gained momentum—its green mossy fur rippling in waves as it closed in—Milton realized he had, indeed, abandoned all hope.

He stopped, panting, then dropped to his knees. As he held his head in his hands, weeping, he was engulfed by the creature's shadow. Milton stared into the Boogeyperson's big red glowing eye as it scrutinized him. *Get it over with,* thought Milton as the creature grinned with its plastic yellow teeth.

The Boogeyperson lifted off its fake head while

Milton gulped, trying to prepare himself for the hideous demon within. Only instead of a rotting reptile with eyes like curdled pus, this demon had a face like a spooky, spotted china doll with a stringy mop of damp blue hair.

"Boo!" Marlo said while holding her Boogeyperson head by her side.

Milton collapsed with relief, though quickly inflated again with anger.

"Did you *really* have to do that?"

"Yes," Marlo said with a chuckle. "I'm afraid I did."

Marlo wiped a trickle of sweat away from where her eyebrow would have been had she not taken to meticulously plucking them into nonexistence.

"Phew . . . it's hot in this thing," she gasped. "Or maybe I have *boogey* fever!"

Marlo did a little dance that she thought was the Hustle. It wasn't.

Milton looked around nervously. "Let's take your freaky dance party somewhere else. C'mon."

They crept toward the bungle gym and reunited with Virgil.

"Milton!" he said with fleeting joy. "And a Boogeyman!"

Virgil backed toward the clubfoot house—a large, ramshackle play structure that leaned drastically toward the bungle gym on one side—and whimpered.

Marlo knelt down and poked her clearly Marlo-ish head into the play structure.

"It's Boogey*person*," Marlo said calmly. "And it's just me, dork."

Virgil's fear abated into simple, manageable unease.

"It's just that," he gasped, "that costume is so . . . so terrifying!"

Milton and Marlo grinned at each other as Virgil crept out of the clubfoot house cautiously.

"H-how?" he stammered. "How did you get here? In that . . . *costume*?"

"Here," she said, straightening herself. "I'll show you."

She put her Boogey head back on (much to Virgil's distress) and led them toward the KinderScare center.

"In case anyone sees us," she whispered through the airhole in her wide, grinning mouth, "act like you're my prisoners or something."

That should be easy, Milton thought. He always felt like Marlo's prisoner anyway.

Milton's backpack writhed and jerked furiously.

"What's the deal with Lucky?" Marlo asked.

"I don't know," replied Milton with concern. "He's not himself lately."

They arrived at the smudgy glass at the center's entrance.

"The short, movie-trailer version is," Marlo explained, "that there were guards, a brilliant performance by yours truly, a visit to the nurse, and a little trade."

Marlo smiled—which of course no one could see, but Milton, after years of exposure, could sense it nonetheless—and gestured toward KinderScare.

Through the daubs of snot and smears of paste, Milton could see the rows of gingerbread coffins quaking in jerky spasms. Inside, Boogeypeople, tied up with black licorice and gagged with pocked Nerf balls and used Band-Aids, fought to free themselves as crazed toddlers danced spastically around them. The children waved flash cards with letter combinations on them while overmouthing vowels.

"Look at them," Milton muttered. "They've got their phonics fix and they're totally out of control."

Milton turned toward his sister, trying to conceal his respect for her apparent success. "How'd you pull it off?" he asked.

Marlo puffed up, her green, shaggy Boogeyperson chest swelling.

"It was an inside job," Marlo said, gesturing toward little Julius, who was bouncing like a ball, savoring every sweet diphthong.

"I gave a signal to my little friend to create a disturbance," Marlo continued matter-of-factly. "And while the nurse and assorted Boogeyfolk were occupied, I picked the lock to that chest all the phonics freaks are obsessed with and created my very own vowel movement. And I don't think the Boogeypeople are too happy about it . . ."

The three children stared at the shuddering ginger-bread coffins and the creatures therein. The bound demons wriggled with rage.

"Even though we're in Limbo," Milton said, "I don't think we have a lot of time."

"Stage Two?" chirped Virgil.

"Yep," Milton said gravely. "Okay, does everyone know what they're supposed to do?"

The Fauster children both stared at Virgil.

"What?" he replied defensively. "I know what to do . . . sneak into Mr. Dior's office where they keep all of our old clothes, and stitch together our soul balloon."

Marlo nodded. "Good. Don't screw this up. Without you, this plan literally will not fly."

"You can depend on me," Virgil said earnestly as he placed his fleshy hand on Marlo's shoulder.

Marlo's eyes trained upon Virgil's hand. She shook off his touch with two sharp shakes.

"No touching," Marlo scolded softly.

Virgil cowered back a step.

"Right. Yes. Sorry."

"Anyway," Milton said, desperate to keep the plan from derailing before it even left the station, "after Marlo and I grab as many jars as we can, we'll meet at the gates and wait for them to open."

Virgil nodded. Milton noticed his new friend was trembling.

"Where are we going?" Milton said with a motivating clap of his hands.

"The Surface!" Marlo and Virgil replied in unison.

"When are we getting there?"

"Real soon!"

"Okay, then," Milton said soberly. "Let's do it."

Virgil wiped away a budding tear and headed down the hallway toward Mr. Dior's office.

Marlo reattached her Boogey head and led Milton down the creepy corridor leading to the Assessment Chamber. It was different from the other hallways, Milton thought. The white marble corridor seemed as if it had been here way before Heck was even conceived, an ancient passage that the architects of this awful place had to build around.

"Hopefully they're off duty," Milton whispered as his sister shuffled him along.

"If they aren't," Marlo asserted behind her row of bright yellow teeth, "just follow my lead."

As they approached the great door, Milton felt as if his very essence was slowly sliding down the insides of his body like spiritual honey, and gradually leaking out of the soles of his feet.

Milton drew in a deep breath as his shaking hand touched the doorknob. *Once I go in,* he thought, *there's no turning back. I either come out with an armload of other people's lost souls, or empty-handed and lost—without mine.*

38 · SOUL SEARCHING

THE SQUEAK OF the ancient hinges reverberated through the massive chamber.

"So much for surprise," Milton said.

The round room was as still as a photograph. The atmosphere hung thick and heavy. Everything felt denser here, as if twice the normal amount of molecules were forced to crowd into the same space.

"Hello?" Marlo called in a poor approximation of a leathery demon voice. "Boogeyperson here on official Heck business."

Marlo looked around through her big red eye.

"Looks dead in here," she murmured. She scanned the rows of glass jars housing writhing, ectoplasmic goop. "Let's go shopping."

As they walked softly across the gleaming floor, they heard a big wet yawn.

Coiled on a round satin pillow beneath the scales on the sunken stage, Annubis raised his long, dignified head. He stretched languidly, resembling a shaved, oversized greyhound clad in a spotless white tunic. After sniffing the air with his moist snout, he gradually opened his soulful eyes.

"Milton," he said majestically in a voice like dark rumpled velvet.

It was hard to explain what hearing his name coming out of the dog god's mouth felt like exactly. But Milton knew the effect had made it impossible for him to lie. Annubis's probing gaze was like a mental and emotional X-ray.

"We . . . we . . . ," Milton stammered. Marlo poked him in the back with her paw, knocking her brother's voice back into groove like one of her father's old jazz records. "We came to get some of the jars," he continued.

Annubis rose. His limbs unfolded and he became terribly tall and terribly thin. The half man, half hound was the only thing that seemed to fit this imposing hall of marble and gold.

"The jars," Marlo added in her creaky Boogey-person voice. "Principal Bubb wanted us to collect the lost souls and take them to her office. She said she found some secret use for them."

Annubis sniffed the air suspiciously. Just then an

ivory chest adorned with silver inlays of smiling bunny skeletons that was next to the dog god began to shake. The lid slid off and landed with a clatter on the gold floor of the stage. Out rose Ammit from a bed of dry ice.

"What is going on?" he croaked in a voice gurgling with phlegm.

Annubis never once took his eyes off Milton. The stately creature had been, during their last encounter, something of a friend, albeit, a friend who reached into your etheric body and plucked out your soul. Milton simply couldn't read him—and Milton could read just about anything.

"They want to take some of the jars of lost souls," Annubis said slowly. "Miss Fauster says that Principal Bubb has found a secret use for them."

"That's right," Marlo croaked. "We . . . wait, I'm not . . ."

Marlo's voice faltered as she stammered between her real voice and poor Boogeyperson imitation.

Milton swallowed. He and his sister squeezed hands.

"The nose knows," Annubis said, sensing their confusion and discomfiture.

Marlo whispered to Milton.

"I say we grab as many as we can and make a break for it."

Annubis scratched himself behind the ear.

"I heard that of course, and—for your sakes—I wouldn't recommend it."

"I thought dogs were a man's best friend," Marlo muttered.

Ammit coughed, jiggling his gelatinous bulk in rippling waves. He rubbed his chin dubiously.

"This must be some kind of test," he carped. "Principal Bubb must have put them up to it."

Annubis trod gracefully toward Milton and Marlo. "I would like to help you," he said with glum sincerity. "Truly I would. But I can't."

His hangdog face surveyed the wall of countless jars, each containing a glistening, restless spiritual essence.

"If a dog god is anything, he's loyal to his master," Annubis continued. "Besides, if those souls were released, there would be chaos. If even one of them reached the Surface, it would break the Prime Defective."

"What's that?" Milton asked while inching furtively toward the wall.

Ammit scratched himself in a place just south of proper. "It's an unshakable statute," he said while the remains of his last meal plopped farther down his transparent digestive tract. "An edict. The rule of rules. In short, it strictly forbids anyone or anything disturbing the queue of souls either entering or exiting the Stage."

Ammit grew agitated. "I don't have time for this," he said, sloshing toward his headset lying between the scales of justice. "Whether this is a drill or an act of insurrection, I need to call Principal Bubb stat."

Marlo nudged her brother.

"This isn't working. It's time for Plan B."

"Plan B?" Milton replied apprehensively. "*What* Plan B?"

Marlo took off her Boogeyperson head and cleared her throat.

"Kum ba yah, my Lord, kum ba yah!
Kum ba yah, my Lord, kum ba yah!"

Oh no, Milton thought as he clapped his hands over his ears. *Not singing.* Anything *but Marlo's singing.*

"Kum ba yah, my Lord, kum ba yah!
O Lord, kum ba yah!"

Annubis's ears drooped. He hunched over and twirled in tight, nervous circles.

Marlo straightened and raised her terrible, screeching, nails-on-a-chalkboard voice.

"Hear me singing, Lord, kum ba yah!
Hear me singing, Lord, kum ba yah!"

A faint, dopey smile creased Ammit's face as he sat placidly down on his ivory chest. Annubis, however, was anything but tranquil. His eyes trained on Marlo, Annubis snarled and licked flecks of foam from his quavering lips and took one staggering step forward.

"Hear me singing, Lord, kum ba yah!
O Lord . . ."

Milton nudged his sister sharply in the ribs.

"Okay, Plan B gets an 'F.' Now what?"

Marlo was oblivious as she strained to hit frightened notes that tried desperately and successfully to elude her unique vocal stylings.

"Ms. Von Trapp said this song soothed demons," she said in between breaths.

The growling dog god pawed closer to the source of his auditory torment.

"Maybe demons," Milton said, licking his dry lips, "but I think it's rubbing *him* the wrong way."

Ammit shook his jelly head and came to his senses.

"This is ridiculous," he said groggily. "I'm calling the principal."

As Annubis, by all appearances consumed by rabies, came within pouncing distance of the Fauster children, Marlo realized that it was time for Plan C, whatever that was.

"Marlo," Milton murmured as he clutched his sister's

shaggy green side, "I never thought I'd say this, but I hope you've got something else up your sleeve."

Up my sleeve, Marlo thought with a jolt of inspiration. She cast aside her Boogeyperson gloves as Annubis, still seized by a temporary madness, stalked closer. Marlo wriggled Ms. Mallon's rib loose from its home, tucked away close to her forearm. She waved the rib over her head.

"Here, doggie!" she cried. "Come get your bone! C'mon . . . who's a good boy? *Annubis* is a good boy!"

Annubis's pupils dilated until they were twin caves of dark, primal want.

"Come get your yum-yum! Mmmm . . . bony bone good!"

The once dignified dog god's jaw dropped open. A river of saliva leaked from his foam-drenched flews. His head followed the arc of the waving bone like a ticking metronome.

Ammit went for his transmitter headset. In the blink of an eye, Milton grabbed the bone from his sister's hand and raced down the descending concentric stairs and landed on the gleaming gold stage.

The quivering blob of goo snatched his headset triumphantly.

Milton roared and—clutching the rib over his head with both sweating hands—brought the bone down hard into Ammit's gaping mouth and deep into his throat.

The creature was startled, stock-still. Unable to

resist his urge to swallow, Ammit gulped the rib down into his visible stomach, where it bobbed provocatively in a sea of bile.

Milton and Ammit turned to see Annubis, skulking down each marble ring, licking his lips and staring at the bone bobbing within the jelly demon.

"Now, now, friend," Ammit rasped while backing away, "let's just take a deep, grounding breath and think this through."

Milton vaulted up the stairs to Marlo's side.

"Quick," he panted, "grab as many as you can."

Marlo smirked with pride at her continually surprising little brother. She and Milton began grabbing jars and dropping them into the Boogeyperson head.

"These are heavy," she said.

Milton, too, struggled with the surprisingly hefty jars.

"I guess they have to be," he grunted, "to keep the souls put . . . I just hope this is enough."

Meanwhile Annubis crept onto the golden stage and eased his weight back on his quivering haunches, ready to spring.

Marlo looked on with fascinated disgust.

"This isn't going to be pretty."

"C'mon!" Milton shouted, and the two children left the chamber, dragging the heavy Boogey head behind them.

The door shut as they fled down the corridor to the clatter and tinkle of jostled jars.

"Bad doggie!" Ammit yelled before his voice was drowned out by a series of savage gulps, growls, and slurps.

Marlo looked over her fuzzy green shoulder.

"Guess there's always room for Jell-O."

39 · A STITCH JUST IN TIME

THE DRESS WAS incredibly tight. So tight that, had Virgil been an actual girl, he very well might have caused a civil disturbance. He crept with surprising grace considering his bulk through Mr. Dior's seemingly endless rows of empty hangers, with the odd negligee, tank top, and jogging suit breaking up the monotony.

Virgil poked his head out between a pair of too-stretched pants and a moth-eaten muumuu.

There, between Virgil and the large tub of sturdy boys' clothing he needed, was Mr. Dior, half asleep and cradling a jug containing (judging by its label) "spirits."

Eerie glowing vapors leaked out of the jug as Mr. Dior took a sleepy swig.

"Ah," he moaned with satisfaction, "phantasmic!"

His bloodshot eyes trained upon Virgil, whose attempt at camouflage would have been more successful had he been surrounded by other two-hundred-pound boys in dresses.

"Either my dressing dummy has gained a few pounds, or I see a naughty little boy who likes to play dress-up."

Virgil gulped, though his budding Adam's apple couldn't quite squeeze past his tight, ruffled collar.

Mr. Dior drooped forward.

"Zere is nothing to be ashamed of, boy," he said with a mischievous smirk. "I myself used to play ze dress-up as a child."

The bald man savaged by scars loosened his silk ascot and beckoned Virgil forward.

"Let me see you."

Virgil, grudgingly, left the imaginary safety of the clothing rack.

"Hello, Mr. Dior," Virgil replied, his chins collapsed tightly to his chest as he looked down at the floor. "I just came to, uh, to get some clothes for a sewing project."

Mr. Dior smiled and crossed his legs primly. "I took ze Stage by storm, with my leetle sewing projects," he reflected groggily.

"Yeah," said Virgil, seeing an opportunity to distract his dapper obstacle. "I think my mom had some of your clothes. So why is a big-time designer like you down here?"

Mr. Dior's face bloomed with a smile. *"Oui,"* he said

with faraway eyes, "I used to be ze French toast of ze town in my day. I made people beautiful."

The plump man heaved a melancholy sigh.

"But, according to ze rules, I helped fan ze flames of vanity and its dark twin, insecurity. So here I am, serving time for my fashion crime."

Virgil eyed the tub of clothes and tried to creep closer. "That is so wrong," he said earnestly.

As Virgil edged nearer, he studied Mr. Dior's jigsaw puzzle of a face, which looked, fittingly, as if it had been stitched together. "How did you get here?"

Mr. Dior rubbed the thick scars that crisscrossed his head. "Vell," he mused, "in ze catty and competitive fashion world, I vuz constantly forced to outdo myself. So I decided to do something unheard of: hold a runway fashion show on a *real* runway, at ze Charles de Gaulle International Airport to be exact! But my nincompoop assistant failed to inform ze airport officials about our dress rehearsal. So as my latest line was making its way down ze runway, a jet plane landed and, vell, I was sucked into ze engine like a bird!"

By this time Virgil was at the tub of boys' clothes, pondering how he could leave with enough to make a decent-sized balloon.

"I see you like those tacky, modern clothes all ze boys had to cast away," Mr. Dior said, snapping out of his reverie.

"I—I was going to—if it is okay with you—use

them to make a, um, new suit," Virgil improvised. "I just find you so *inspiring*."

Mr. Dior glared at Virgil for an uncomfortably long time. Finally, he stood.

"I'm afraid I can't let you do zat," he replied.

Virgil's supersized stomach sunk like a stone. What was even worse than not breaking out of this awful place was the fact that he had let his two friends down.

Mr. Dior stood stout and stern before him.

"Rules are rules: zese tasteless, inelegant rags cannot leave zis room."

He reached deep into his pocket with a look of brooding intensity.

"But," he continued, "zere is no rule zat says zey cannot leave as a jumbo-sized Dior creation!"

Mr. Dior pulled out a long, rusty needle and a spool of catgut thread.

"Ze tools and materials are crude," he said with a smile, "but I am nothing eef not resourceful."

Virgil breathed a deep sigh of relief, and—in the process—burst through his already immodest dress. Mr. Dior shook his head.

"I must hurry," he said. "Time is vasting, and your vaist is spreading. Your clothes are a dictatorship and your body is revolting."

Virgil's face sank sadly.

"Vell," Mr. Dior continued, "you know vat I mean."

40 · A GATE WiTH DESTiNY

MILTON AND MARLO hid behind several deflated hippity-hops and a pair of rocking horses so old they should have been made into rocking glue, and eyed the imposing Gates of Heck. They carefully set down their collection of soul jars and waited.

Milton picked up a jar and pressed his nose against the glass. A speckled black glob rushed at his face, like an angry, man-eating fish.

"A lot of these souls are mostly dark," Milton said worriedly. "They just seem . . . mean and heavy. See how they just kind of sink to the bottom? I hope there are enough of the light, rainbow floaty ones to get us to the Surface."

Marlo looked down the main hallway. "If Virgil doesn't get here soon, it won't really matter."

A metallic squeak pierced through the background

drone of the hallway. Milton and Marlo stared at each other with round, apprehensive eyes.

Through the swirls and eddies of greasy smoke, they could see the glint of some metal . . . *thing* . . . wheeling toward them. As Milton and Marlo tried to make peace with the fact that they would probably soon be captured by some new, awful robot thing, they heard a familiar voice call from the murk.

"Look!" Virgil exclaimed as he wheeled the clothing rack toward the gate. Draped over the rack was a huge patchwork of jeans, T-shirts, and hoodies, stitched together into an enormous shirt. Virgil pulled off the extra-extra-extra-large shirt and showed it to Milton and Marlo.

"I got Mr. Dior to make it," he said with pride. "Then—when he passed out—I sewed up the sleeves and the bottom, so all we have to do is release the souls into the neck, and tie it up with these belts."

Virgil unraveled a coiled mass of belts tied tightly together, then grinned with satisfaction.

"Wow," Marlo said with respect. "You really did it. Not that we doubted you or anything, we just thought you'd screw it up somehow. Nice dress, by the way."

Virgil looked down and blushed.

Milton jabbed Marlo in the ribs. He gave Virgil's hand a hearty shake and patted him on the back. Virgil looked up shyly.

"So far so good," Milton said, "but we're only halfway there."

In ten minutes, they had dragged over a bent, tetanus-rich erector-set structure, several plastic shopping carts with busted wheels, and some foul-smelling Stinker Toys to create a sort of barricade by the gates. The three children crouched behind it and took cover.

"I hate this part," Marlo groused, "Operation Hurry Up, Up, Up and Wait."

"It's either hiding here until another 'guest' drops in and the gates open, or somehow getting Principal Bubb's finger key," Milton whispered.

"I'd like to give *her* the finger," Marlo muttered.

Milton's backpack wriggled and writhed.

"Your ferret sure is freaking out," Virgil said as Milton yanked off the agitated sack.

"What is it, little guy?" Milton cooed softly as he lifted the canvas flap.

Inside, "Lucky" was coiled in the corner, hissing and panting. Milton cautiously felt his way into the bag.

"Oww!" he yelped. "He bit me again! He never did that upstairs!"

Milton wrapped his hands in his sleeves and grabbed the frantic ferret quickly. He trapped him in his lap, using his legs as a vise.

"Wow," Virgil whispered. "It's like he's rabid . . . Hey, what are those?"

Virgil pointed at two large boils on either side of Lucky's neck. Milton cleared away the matted white fur to get a better look.

"His fur's all weird, too," Milton commented with concern. "It's all thick and gross."

He leaned closer to examine the boils. They were big, hard like pebbles, and—*It must be my imagination,* Milton thought—looked like they had tiny faces.

"Whatever they are," Milton said, "they look like they're coming to a head."

"His eyes," Marlo murmured. "Something's wrong with his eyes."

Milton squinted at his supposed pet. "I don't see any . . ."

"Move him around again," Marlo said. "I saw a quick flash of something . . . *There!*"

The three children looked into the fake ferret's gaze.

"Contact lenses?" Milton mumbled.

"Weird," Virgil said. "Does he have bad eyesight or something?"

The Fauster children glared at Virgil, then proceeded to ignore him.

"You can only see them when the light hits them just so," Milton commented.

"He's not going to like this," Marlo whispered as she rolled up her woolly green sleeve. Gently, she pressed her thumb to the surface of Lucky's eye. The creature winced and licked flecks of foam off its raised lips.

Marlo examined the contact lens stuck to the tip of her thumb. "There's, like, a little clear sensor thing in it," she said. "And another tiny lens inside . . . It's like a camera or something."

Milton subdued the struggling animal and removed the second contact-lens camera.

"Maybe that's why he's been acting so weird," Virgil remarked.

"Maybe," Milton said while staring at the lens. "Who knows what that horrible, overbearing beast did to him. Poor guy."

He scratched Lucky behind the ear. The creature spat back a wet, wicked wheeze in reply.

"Here, buddy," Milton said while putting the agitated animal into his knapsack. "Hopefully he'll chill out in there. He must be traumatized."

"And we must be under surveillance," Marlo added.

Marlo peered over their barricade of broken toys. Across the foul playground and inside the KinderScare, she could see a couple of hungry toddlers nibbling through the licorice bonds of the Boogeypeople who lay, livid, inside the gingerbread coffins.

Her pupils grew large and dark as she stared back at the tiny cameras in her hand. Milton watched his sister's face like a movie he had seen so many times he knew it by heart.

"Oh no," he muttered. "Not that look, Marlo. What are you planning . . . I mean, what are you going to do?"

"I'm not sure," Marlo said truthfully. She smiled a spooky grin at her brother. "I never really know until it happens—you know that. You think and never act, I act and never think. That's why we either work really well together, or really bad."

"Badly," Milton corrected.

Marlo grabbed the other contact lens from Milton with a swift swipe. "I can't wait around for some kid upstairs to fall out of his tree house in order for that gate to open. You two stay here. Don't worry about me: I got it covered."

"*Have* it covered," Milton mumbled as his sister lumbered away in her Boogeyperson getup.

"Wait!" Virgil called. Milton stifled Virgil's cry with a cupped hand.

"Shhh!" he hissed. "It's no use. Once her mind's set on something, you'd have an easier time convincing rain to fall up."

Marlo shambled down the hallway leading back toward Bea "Elsa" Bubb's not-so-secret lair. She rounded a bend, then stopped and looked over her fuzzy green shoulder to make sure she was out of Milton's and Virgil's sight. Marlo delicately plucked the contact lenses out of her clammy palm and placed them in her eyes.

"There," she said while blinking the sting out of her eyes. "Operation Goose Chase is a go."

41 · GOOSE PiMPLES

FLAMES SHOT DOWN on Milton and Virgil from the fire sprinklers embedded in the foul playground's low, checkerboard ceiling.

"Marlo," whispered Milton, cringing as he stared at the fire sprinklers flaring angrily between patches of crumbling asbestos.

Virgil was stricken with terror. His wide, quivering eyes flickered with fire and blue strobe lights. He bolted toward the gates.

"Virgil!" yelled Milton. "Don't"—Virgil touched the gates, setting off another alarm—"touch the gates or you'll set off another alarm."

★   ★   ★

"Principal Bubb!" shouted a thin, ropy demon that resembled a twisted pepperoni stick. "Another alarm has gone off, this one at the gates!"

Bea "Elsa" Bubb blinked groggily at the screen in her sleeping cove while removing the curlers from her coarse back hair.

"I got that," she said, yawning, "when my security screen flashed 'Gate Alarm.' Instead of playing newscaster, why don't you try doing your job and see what's going on?"

The living meat stick bowed with shame. "Yes, Principal. Of course. I'll see to—"

The demoness flicked a switch and the screen went black.

"Yadda yadda yadda," she groused as she tightened her whalebone corset. After a series of cracks and creaks, she wriggled into her leather dress, gave her hooves a quick buff, then fished out her surveillance pod from her dwarf-rabbit purse.

"Let me see if my widdle boopsy bottom can shed some light on this."

She rubbed a button with her claw and the device's screen blinked to life. On the small display, she could see the hallway leading to her lair streaking by, blurred with speed.

"Oh, my badness," she gasped. "My little devil is racing for his mama. He must be in trouble!"

Principal Bubb jabbed a candy-like button on her communications console.

"Calling all demon guards! Report at once to my secret lair!"

She darted out of her sleeping cove through her not-so-secret egress and hoofed it into the hallway. The corridor was a circus of flame, flashing lights, and noise. Principal Bubb held the surveillance pod in front of her, letting it guide her like a high-tech compass.

"I'm coming, precious!" she called out as she cantered through the hectic passageway. On the tiny screen she could make out a familiar strip of corridor—one that was just beyond her—around a snaking bend past the custodial supply pit.

"Almost there!" Bea "Elsa" Bubb panted. She screwed up her sickly yellow-green eyes at the blurry display. A dark figure appeared on the screen, trotting through a bank of oily clouds.

Principal Bubb waved smoke away from the screen to get a better look. The figure became more distinct: an attractive creature with a fetching figure and a flattering leather dress. It was holding a tiny surveillance pod. It was . . . *her*.

Principal Bubb stopped in her tracks.

"My precious . . ."

She looked up to see a girl's head sticking out of a Boogeyperson's body. Marlo squeaked to a halt. Her eyes flickered like a red neon sign.

"It's n-nice to see you, t-too," Marlo stammered. "Must have made a wrong turn."

Several demon guards marched through the cloud of smoke, stopping on either side of Marlo. The squad squeezed against her like a vice.

Principal Bubb folded her flabby arms together.

"I assume this will be going on my permanent record," Marlo said with a nervous smirk.

42 · THE BUBB STOPS HERE

THINGS WERE REALLY starting to heat up at the gates. One by one the Boogeypeople were being freed from their licorice bonds by hungry, shortsighted rug rats. Sirens were blaring. Lights were flashing. And Cerberus, still in ferret form, was thrashing about in Milton's backpack. And, despite the countless distractions and the fact that his heart was beating up in his tonsils, Milton's eyes never wavered from the hallway that his sister had entered moments before.

"They must have grabbed her," Virgil said sadly.

Milton shook his head. "It's not fair," he moaned. "We're good kids . . . *mostly* . . . we don't deserve this. This whole place was created to make sure kids like us never get a break. And they've had eternity to perfect every defect."

He stared hopefully at the point he last saw his sister.

"I feel like if I just want to see her bad . . . *badly* . . . enough, she'll suddenly appear."

At that moment, Marlo waddled through the dense whorl of smoke, her arms behind her back. Milton laughed with relief, until he saw a squat, shadowy figure emerge just behind her.

"Sorry, bro," Marlo murmured sadly. "This wild goose got chased, plucked, and cooked."

Principal Bubb shoved Marlo forward.

"Back off, Bubb," Marlo spat, twisting toward her captor.

Milton could see that tightly coiled anaconda cuffs bound his sister's wrists and ankles.

Bea "Elsa" Bubb shoved Marlo toward the gate. Marlo looked apologetically at Milton and Virgil.

"I tried to buy you some time," she said with a shrug of her shaggy Boogeyperson shoulders.

Milton smiled sadly. "What you should've bought was that stupid oar."

Marlo grinned back at him, though tears fell down her cheeks. "Why would I buy an oar?" she said with a catch in her throat. "We lived in Kansas, short bus."

Principal Bubb sighed impatiently.

Milton stared anxiously at the gate, waiting for a new guest to open the portal between this life and the last.

A dozen or so gnarled prune bananas with pitch-sporks came running down the hallway from the demon depot. As they rounded the corner, they tumbled like jumbo-sized dominos on the slick, freshly swabbed floor.

Bea "Elsa" Bubb rolled her beady eyes at the impromptu game of Slip 'n' Slide.

"*Blackbeard,*" she seethed under her breath. The principal puffed up her chest like an especially ugly blowfish.

"Regardless, Mr. Fauster, you and your hapless accomplices are up the River Styx without a paddle."

At that moment something small, white, and furry scurried between the nasty goat legs of the ancient demoness.

"Lucky?" Milton exclaimed.

The animal skidded to a halt and, with a squeak, rushed at Milton and hopped into his arms.

"But . . . aren't you in my . . . ?"

The ferret sniffed the air, then ran over Milton's shoulder and burrowed into his knapsack. The bag writhed, squealed, and hissed. Milton yanked off the knapsack and dropped it on the ground. He unbuckled the straps and two ferocious, screeching tubes of vicious fur tumbled out. End over end, they rolled in savage combat.

"Precious!" Principal Bubb yelped, her curdled eyes wide with alarm.

The two wounded, nappy, disheveled creatures broke their death grip and circled each other, panting and hissing.

"It's like that old *Star Trek* episode," Milton mumbled, "where the transporter split Kirk into an evil Kirk and a good Kirk, and Spock had to decide which was which."

"Well," Virgil replied, "maybe the good one is the ferret with the dice around its neck, and the bad one is the ferret crawling with blisters and growing two extra heads."

"Cerberus?" Milton uttered softly. "But how?"

It dawned on him that the fuzzy white abomination thrashing between him and the Principal of Darkness was a bargaining chip, something that held the potential to tilt matters in Milton's favor.

Principal Bubb lurched forward. Marlo hopped in front of her. Milton ran at Lucky and Cerberus and scooped them up.

"Lucky!" Milton called as his true pet licked his salty face with abandon.

"Okay, okay. Nice to see you, too," Milton said soothingly. *"Knapsack."*

Lucky scrambled up and over his master's shoulder and burrowed into the knapsack.

Milton clutched Cerberus by the scruff of his middle neck. He held the shape-shifting creature out, squirming in front of him.

"I think I have something you want," Milton said to the principal calmly.

Bea "Elsa" Bubb rose from the ground with a labored grunt. Milton studied her face. He could see her holding back spasms of alarm and concern.

"You couldn't hurt a fly," she said through gritted teeth. "I saw your file. I know who you are. You're nothing."

Milton looked straight into her rancid yolk eyes. "Virgil, get me a jar," he said through the side of his mouth. "One with lots of those nasty black bits."

Virgil grabbed the blackest, stormiest jar he could find and stood next to Milton.

Bea "Elsa" Bubb swallowed. "You wouldn't dare," she jeered.

Milton gave Virgil a faint nod. Virgil struggled to unscrew the jar's lid, and—after much exertion—was rewarded with a twist. The dark, vicious soul glob lunged to the top, shuddering in angry spasms. Milton swung Cerberus over to the jar.

"If you want 'precious' back, then open the gates. If not, Cerberus here has a playdate with the little soul piranha."

Bea "Elsa" Bubb stood as still as a gargoyle on top of an old library. "Fine," she said with barely contained rage. "Have it your way."

Virgil's stomach growled. *"Have it your way,"* he murmured with longing.

Principal Bubb strutted over to the majestic Gates of Heck and extended her intricately manicured index claw. She stuck it into the keyhole and gave it a twist.

The sirens stopped suddenly. The Gates of Heck

creaked open. Every squeak, every grating rasp echoed in the profound silence.

"There," Principal Bubb said. The word was like a brick of ice that fell to the ground and shattered the second it was uttered. "You are free to go . . . You'd be the first."

Now that Milton had bluffed his way this far, he didn't know what to do.

"The gates are open, Mr. Fauster," she said. "I've kept my end of the bargain, now it's time to keep yours."

"Don't!" Marlo yelped.

Milton glanced over his shoulder at Virgil. "Let's get busy with the jars."

Virgil nodded and tried desperately to unscrew the lids. Milton stepped forward and took a deep breath.

"M-my sister," he faltered. "Let her . . . let her go."

"Oh, Mr. Fauster," the principal chortled. "We all know that isn't going to happen."

Marlo hobbled closer to Milton.

"I'm the one that belongs here," Marlo snuffled. "You were just collateral damage."

The guards, after several unsuccessful tries, had finally managed to right themselves on the slick floor. Bea "Elsa" Bubb gave them an unspoken order with her eyes.

One of Cerberus's heads nipped the back of Milton's hand.

"Fine!" yelped Milton as he let the wriggling creature drop to the ground. As soon as its half ferret, half dog paws touched the floor, Cerberus darted away.

"Sweetums!!" Principal Bubb gushed as Cerberus leapt into her arms.

Marlo shook her head sadly.

"Oh, Milton . . . why?"

"I'm a boy of my word," he said plainly. "It may not mean much here, but it means a lot to me."

Cerberus licked his true master's face until it was slick with slobber.

"You can keep your words," the Principal Bubb tittered.

She jabbed the underside of one of her bracelets, sort of a blinking glass bone formed around her wrist studded with jewel-like buttons. The Gates of Heck began to scrape closed.

"Guards!" Principal Bubb shouted.

Suddenly the bell tolled for a new arrival.

Barely after the gates had closed, the majestic entrance once again rumbled open.

"If you've lived a life so bad . . . ," sang the lounge lizards as they scrambled onto their dinky stage.

Principal Bubb's fleshy jowls sagged down in surprise. She jabbed her wrist control, but the doors spread wide in creaking disregard.

"I can't override!" she barked desperately. "The main portal is on automatic."

"Virgil!" Milton yelped. "The jars!"

The enormous boy's face was flushed with exertion.

"It's hard," he wheezed. "Most of the lids just won't budge, and they're all so heavy."

"Smash them open," Milton yelled, "and herd them inside the balloon!"

Virgil nodded and began to shatter jar after jar with a tire-less Tonka truck. The souls wriggled free. Frantically Virgil scooped them into the quilted blimp.

The balloon rippled to life. Yet, after a moment, most of the living lumps clung to the bottom, while precious few billowed to the top.

Virgil peeked inside the balloon.

"The black ones are just trying to bite the sides . . . Oww!" Virgil yelped after a dark soul glob went for his eye. "The happy colorful ones are soaring . . . or would if there were just more of them."

Milton ran to his side and started smashing the dwindling collection of jars.

"*Today*, guards!" barked Principal Bubb.

Three demons charged toward Milton and Virgil. Panicked, Milton thrust his hand in a mostly black jar and grabbed a fistful of the nasty, squirming things. They felt like jiggling, electric snot. He winced with pain as the soul bits pinched, stung, and chomped on his hand with unseen teeth.

With a scream, Milton hurled the wriggling globs

at the guards. They swarmed around them like flying jellyfish—with the intent, or so it seemed, of entering them.

Virgil cracked open the last jar, freeing a glistening, multihued soul that rushed into the balloon to join the buoyant flock of similarly sparkling light creatures. They nuzzled and cooed like doves.

The balloon rose higher as Milton siphoned out more of the black globs that, once free, streamed out like fat, angry bits of phlegm. Principal Bubb and her guards danced around in spasmodic terror, swatting the tormenting blobs. The dark whizzing bits swooped inside demonic ears, noses, or mouths, then swiftly rushed out to find new victims.

Milton helped Virgil to cinch off the end of the balloon with the knotted-together belts.

The demons had captured Marlo and were now hoisting her into the air like a small crowd at a rock concert catching a stage diver. She writhed angrily and bit anything that came near her pearly white fangs.

"Marlo!" Milton yelled at the top of his lungs.

"Go!" she screamed hysterically. "I'm toast!"

Milton cringed at the word "toast." The balloon lurched toward the portal.

"It's now or never!" Virgil grunted as he tried to restrain the floating wardrobe.

Milton saw Damian's head peeking out at the edge of the dancing mass of demons. He locked eyes with

Milton, straightened his tie, and parted the crowd like Moses gone bad.

Milton and Virgil maneuvered the restless balloon through the gates, toward the coiling slide.

Damian fought his way through the attacking swarm while Principal Bubb swatted maniacally in all directions. She lost her balance and fell on her plump, bristly butt. "Get them, you useless, dried-up strips of road kill!" she screeched.

Meanwhile, Virgil and Milton were leaping into the air, hoping that their balloon would follow suit.

"It's . . . no . . . use," panted Virgil.

Milton hunkered down in an attempt to achieve more "spring."

"We just need . . . to jump higher," Milton replied, steadfast. "C'mon, put some altitude in your attitude."

Virgil huffed and puffed and blew his hopes down.

"I don't think my . . . attitude is ever . . . going to break the law of . . . gravity."

Damian grabbed a pitchspork from an addled demon. He cut a swath through the chaos and stopped just outside the gates.

"There's hardly any sport in this," Damian said, hoisting the pitchspork over his head and behind his shoulder, ready to launch. "But it's not how you play the game, it's if you win or lose that counts."

Milton locked eyes with Damian.

Perhaps it was the exhaustion, or the hunger that

gnawed his insides, or the itchy wool pajamas. Whatever it was, Milton had been pushed too far. In this moment, a spring of bubbling rage washed away the fear that had clung to Milton like moss on a rock ever since he could remember.

"Then get it over with, you gutless twerp!" Milton shouted.

Damian's pupils widened until his eyes were twinkling lumps of angry coal. His nostrils flared like bellows, fanning the smoldering rage within.

"Aaaarrrrggghhh!!" he roared as he hurled the pitchspork with deadly accuracy toward Milton's chest.

Before Milton even had a chance to react, an eight-year-old boy came tumbling down the slide, head over heels, and fell onto the soul balloon. The balloon pitched forward and absorbed the business end of Damian's pitchspork.

Milton and Virgil toppled over into the pool of Ping-Pong balls and garbage, still clutching the belts strapped to their flight-shy balloon.

"Lucky break," muttered Virgil. He looked over at the stunned boy. He was wearing a torn T-shirt that read "I Nearly Survived Unbalanced Bill's Fork 'n Toaster Roller Coaster!" "Well, for us, anyway," Virgil added.

Milton looked upward at the hissing ball of stitched-together clothes that he and Virgil held tethered. There was a gash in between a pair of navy blue corduroys and a plaid pajama top. Though the tear was only a few inches wide, white blobs of soul were squirming out of the balloon, causing it to sag slightly on one side.

Milton, too, seemed to sag at the sight. Virgil gazed at the gash, then back at his despondent friend. A sad smile crept across his face.

"If anyone deserves a lucky break, it's you," he said with a gleam in his eye. "I'm just holding you back."

Milton cocked his head at his largest and best friend in this or any world.

"What are you talking . . . ?"

Virgil untangled his arm from the line of knotted belts until he held the very end with his fist. He looked over at Damian, who was just inside the gates with a baffled expression plastered across his face.

"You know what?" Virgil asked Damian warmly.

"What?" Damian grudgingly responded.

Virgil smiled. "Chicken butt!"

Virgil let go of the belt. The balloon—and Milton—rushed up through the portal toward the Surface.

"No!!!" yelled Milton as he soared upward.

Tears leaked down Virgil's smiling face.

"Send down a triple cheeseburger!" he hollered as a furious Damian and several demon guards pressed through the gates to seize him.

The whole scene shrank down to a feverish dot of activity as Milton rose up, up and away. The last thing Milton could make out was Marlo's unmistakable voice cutting through the rush of wind.

"Way to go, bro!! What an exit!! Get your nasty meat hooks off me, you overgrown piece of bologna . . ."

Then it was gone. All Milton could hear was the deafening roar of blowing air. It was like being caught in a vertical wind tunnel, or like skydiving in reverse.

The spiral slide uncoiled both above and below him. Due to his supersonic flight upward, the slide looked like a spinning drill boring through the earth.

Whizzing past were several more children—two little boys and an older girl—racing down the slide. They were wearing the same Fork 'n Toaster Roller Coaster shirt as the little boy below. The three children waved their arms straight up into the air.

"Woo-hoo!" they squealed in delight.

"What a rush!" the oldest boy yelled before disappearing down into the abyss.

After what seemed like hours but was, again, no time at all, Milton rose swiftly toward a bright, ever-expanding opening above him. He felt like a bubble floating to the surface of the ocean. But a bubble's life tends to be short-lived, with a nasty habit of popping upon reaching its destination.

43 · BODY SLAM

MILTON SHUT HIS eyes as he shot out of the portal bridging here and there, up and down, living and dead. With the sudden explosion of noise and light, Milton felt as if he were being born a second time.

He finally got the courage to open his eyes. Beneath him lay the gnarled wreckage of a roller coaster—a five-story chrome toaster, with a looping track going in and out of the structure's smoldering slots. At the center of the twisted, smoldering metal and scattered fork-shaped cars was a small, swirling pinwheel of energy. A crowd of parents and children gawked at the debris, yet no one seemed to notice the churning eddy of crackling light. Then, in the blink of an eye, it was gone.

Whizzing upward and outward, Milton noticed a billboard several miles beyond the Fork 'n Toaster Roller Coaster disaster that read UNBALANCED BILL'S

Up, up and away, my beautiful, my beautiful . . .

The balloon above him rustled and jerked. Gliding above the surface of the world, the soul bits became crazed and restless, making their canvas cage seem like a bag of possessed microwave popcorn.

With several vicious dips, fits, and jerks, the balloon ripped apart. The squirming, speckled souls rushed out in every direction.

Milton's stomach tingled and scurried up into his throat as he tumbled earthward. Then another peculiar sensation overtook him. It felt as if there were invisible electric hooks in Milton's heart and head, tugging him relentlessly toward the horizon. The terrain below his feet was now not only hurtling toward him—or so it seemed—but it was also whooshing away. He was indeed being pulled—or propelled—*somewhere*.

Milton's knuckles were white from squeezing hold of the braided belt straps. Now it was like a long, tangled rip cord that led to, instead of a parachute, scraps of mismatched laundry.

Milton looked down. The ground below was strangely *un*strange. Flat, hopeless, monotonous, dreary, devoid of all personality . . .

He was home. Or close to it. The tugging sensation in his chest and head was fierce. It was as if he were trying to reel in two large, spirited fish.

He plunged faster now, toward a drab collection of gray boxes, with blinking trucks outside . . . Grizzly Mall! The parking lot was teeming with people, some crying, some gawking, while others simply milled about like stunned ghosts. A dozen or so, Milton could now see, were caked with smoldering marshmallow.

The crowd parted as two men in white wheeled a stretcher toward an ambulance. On the gurney was a figure . . . a boy . . . He was wearing khaki pants and a navy blue shirt that were mottled with lumps of molten marshmallow. He wore broken glasses. Milton rushed faster toward the boy, the boy who was deathly still, the boy with the sticky, smoking mop of hair. He could see the boy's face, hidden behind a mask of burnt sugar. Milton felt like he was falling into a mirror. Closer, faster, closer, faster. Milton's ears buzzed with a high-pitched whine. The boy . . . *the boy* . . . he could see him perfectly now. The boy was . . .

Milton's etheric body slammed into his lifeless physical one. The pain was incredible. He could feel each and every sleepy atom roughly shoved aside to make room for bristling energy. The noise was deafening. Harsh, stabbing beams of sunlight pressed through his eyelids. The smell was overpowering. Sweet, sickening, sharp, bitter. He could taste it. The taste! It prickled on his tongue, scrambled up the roof of his mouth, then burrowed down his throat. But most of all, he hurt. Everywhere. Dull throbs, rolling aches, spiky twinges, small patches of searing agony. And a great heaviness. It was like he was swaddled in blankets of lead. He felt thick and complicated. He itched. He burned. He tickled. It was like when your foot falls asleep and slowly comes to, only everywhere, inside and out. But at the bottom of it all, at the very foundation, his core, he felt . . . *familiar*. His head throbbed, his heart boiled. Small storms of electricity seethed within him, particles rubbing together, chaffing, sparking, until suddenly, there was a great clap of thunder.

44 · A NEW LEASE
ON DEATH

MILTON BOLTED UPRIGHT on the gurney. The medics jumped back with shock. The crowd screamed as one. Some women fainted. Some men, too.

Milton's into-body experience was overwhelming . . . though that wasn't the right word (and Milton knew most every word). It was beyond the capacity of language to describe.

A great calm gripped the crowd. Suddenly Milton's body reacted to the experience the only way it knew how. It began to weep. Uncontrollably and inconsolably. As oceans of tears gushed out of his eyes, Milton felt as though he would never stop crying. He bawled. He wailed. His body convulsed, wracked with heavy, syrupy sobs.

Through the stinging salt of tears, Milton tried to rein in his emotions with self-analysis. He wasn't crying from grief, he surmised, but from the pure joy of being alive. The air now tasted sweet. The sun caressed his skin with its warmth. The wind felt cool and invigorating . . . *alive.* His lungs swelled pleasantly in his chest. His heart's beat was a steady, thrumming thrill.

The tense calm of the crowd was broken as another blanketed form was wheeled out into the parking lot. The only sound was the steady squeak and low, gravelly rumble of wheels on pavement.

The gurney wheeled closer. The blanket looked like a snow-covered mountain range in miniature. Then Milton looked closer and saw something else. Something terrible. Poking out from between the sheets was a black granny boot. Vintage. Smoldering. And completely still, inanimate, like a doll's shoe.

Though his tear ducts were raw, fresh waves of stinging water leaked out of his eyes. These tears were different. This was sheer, wrenching grief, dredged from deep inside him. This experience had dug a well inside Milton to a place within he never knew existed. A place miles below. *A place . . .*

Milton sniffed back his sorrow and wiped the snot clean from his chin. His descent into Heck. That terrible, confounding, maddening, awful place. Was it real?

A dream? Some severe, trauma-induced nightmare? The result of a highly active imagination combined with near-death hypoxia, leeching his young mind of oxygen, starving his brain into conjuring horrifying, outlandish delusions?

As Milton pondered his sanity among a crowd of shaken onlookers, his knapsack—sticky, black, and smoky—rustled beside him.

Between the flaps nudged a pink, wet, twitching nose. Lucky wriggled out into the sunlight. He winced and shivered, looking shaken and exposed, as if he had just been born again, too.

He surged up Milton's limp arm and onto his chest. Milton grinned through his tears. Lucky crawled to Milton's face and licked it frantically with his nimble little tongue, tickling the boy's chin. Milton giggled and stroked his pet so hard that Lucky gave his master's hand gentle nips.

After a series of scratches and strokes, Lucky grew stock-still. He looked imploringly at Milton with bulging pink eyes and started to undulate. His fur rippled in waves. His neck arched and jerked. Several wet heaves later, Lucky had thrown up all over Milton.

Great, just great, thought Milton. *Just what I need: hot ferret vomit all over me.*

Then Milton saw it: wet pieces of paper floating

in the bile. Scraps with elegantly written words like "indenture," "Soul Holder," and "legally binding covenant." It was a contract . . . *his* contract . . . with that fat, ugly, wretched toad of a she-demon Bea "Elsa" Bubb . . . Principal Bubb!

Milton just had to laugh. It felt like he was crying with his mouth. He couldn't stop. Everything seemed so . . . ridiculous and tragic at the same time.

Lucky had smuggled out Milton's contract with the Powers That Be Evil in his own uniquely ferret-like way.

He looked over at the stretcher with Marlo's cloaked body, surrounded by grim paramedics shaking their heads.

His sister was dead, Milton thought. But she was also, somehow, alive. And the thought of Marlo kicking demons with her etheric legs made him smile.

"All true," he mumbled.

"What was that?" a paramedic with stubble and kind blue eyes asked, leaning closer to him.

Milton stared deeply into his eyes with a hollow sadness.

"You wouldn't understand," he murmured. "No one on earth would."

Lucky burped, and that awful fishy smell dragged Milton back to the parking lot, and the crowd, and the questions that were ready to leap from everyone's lips.

He couldn't bother with this right now. It wasn't

important. Milton swung his singed legs over the stretcher, overcome with a sense of urgency. That nine-ring circus down south was real, and Milton was the only living person to know, *really* know, that it was there.

He hopped off the gurney and swayed. The paramedic steadied him.

"Son, you need to lie back down. You've been through an incredible ordeal."

"You don't know the half of it," Milton said in a spooky whisper while strapping on his backpack.

He staggered across the parking lot as the stunned crowd backed away, making him a path.

Milton could only manage a few steps at a time. He stopped, seized by an incredible vertigo. It was more than dizziness. It was as if he was out of phase with himself. It was like that game where you try to tilt the little steel ball into the hole. Part of Milton was trying to fit back into itself.

"My sentient body," Milton mumbled.

The weird, electrical glue holding me together, he mused while patting his body, trying to make himself somehow more real. *It's . . . gone. Dispersed and absorbed into . . . what was it? The Transdimensional Power Grid?*

Then, as quickly as his etheric body had slid out of his physical one, Milton was whole again. But it was an uneasy feeling. The more Milton concentrated on holding himself together, the more intact he felt. But he knew he couldn't maintain that focus for much longer. He would just have to accept that he would never quite be himself again.

The crowd gawked at Milton as if he were a zombie back from the dead. *An astute observation,* he mused.

Milton shut his eyes in exhaustion as his head swam with sirens, sobs, blurry images, and confounding legal phrases. Cutting through the noise like a cold, blunt knife was Bea "Elsa" Bubb's leathery laugh. It echoed through his consciousness, seeped into his bones, and tormented his very soul.

Just the thought of her made Milton's blood boil. And it actually felt good. It felt real.

And for the first time in his life—and death—Milton enjoyed being different. He felt free: free from caring what people thought, free to choose his own path, free to do something that no boy—dead or alive—had ever done before.

He shuffled past the parking lot and crunched through a playground covered with wood chips toward a swing set. Milton had no idea where to go. He didn't feel like going home. There would need to be too many . . . explanations. And no one would believe—or want to know, really—the truth. But the truth was all he had.

Lucky climbed out of the backpack and into Milton's arms. *Okay,* Milton smiled. *Maybe I do* have a little more *than just the truth.* He had his ferret, he had himself, and he had a mission.

A smile crept over his face as he settled down on a swing. He gently rocked back and forth, feeling the silky arms of sleep wrap around him.

All our days are numbered, he thought before drifting off into unconscious bliss, *but that number is infinity.*

BACKWORD

No matter how far you go, you can never quite get away from yourself. We're our own punishment, our own reward.

Every moment of every day, we decide our fate. We think we have a choice—and we do in a way—but what we have to choose from has been decided long ago. All of our lives—our past lives, present lives, and post lives—are like a big chessboard. It's more than infinite, stretching both backward and forward until it meets itself. It's also terribly wide. And deep. And has a strange smell, kind of like pancakes.

Mmm . . . pancakes.

Deep down in Heck, far beyond the smell of pancakes, the game plays itself out, move by move, pawns advancing, oblivious to the forces that propel them. But someone—or something—has changed the rules. There was a new piece on the chessboard that shouldn't have been there. And now, even though it's gone, it's still in play. A mistake has been made. Or has it?

Sometimes life is a joke that you don't understand: you laugh but you're not sure why. In the afterlife, no one is laughing. Especially those who think the rules are theirs to make. This time the joke is on them.

Ha!

ACKNOWLEDGMENTS

The book in your hands, or that is leaning against your knee, or that a servant is holding up to your face—flipping the pages carefully with gloved fingers—wouldn't have been possible without the complete lack of support of the following persons:

The countless boys (and occasional girl) who—because of untreated glandular conditions, earlier-than-reasonable growth spurts, or simple lack of parental affection—made my life a living heck through bullying, name-calling, psychological torment, or gross failure to appreciate my obvious superiority.

The teachers, school administrators, and after-school athletic "supervisors" who aided the above group—either knowingly or unwittingly—in their pre-pubescent reign of thuggery, manipulation, and almost surgically precise teasing.

The hungry machine we call society that both feeds off and perpetuates the above behavior.

I'd also like to thank my parents, both living and

not-so-living, who supported me to a fault; my wife, Diana, for her faultless support; and my editor, Diane Landolf (no relation), who somehow convinced Random House that publishing a book about dead children was a sound business decision.

ABOUT THE AUTHOR

DALE E. BASYE has written stories, essays, reviews, and lies for many publications and organizations. He was a film critic, winning several national journalism awards, and the publisher of an arts and entertainment newspaper called *Tonic*. He once jumped out of a plane for a story (a story about jumping out of a plane). Luckily, he's never written about brain surgery.

Here's what Dale has to say about his first book:

"There is a time that chafes against childhood and adulthood, leaving a rash that never quite goes away. Sometimes it itches uncontrollably, and no one can see it. It's like when you wear swim trunks for too long out of the pool. Heck is like that. And no matter what anyone tells you, Heck is real. This story is real. Or as real as anything like this can be."

Dale E. Basye lives in Portland, Oregon, as part of the criminal witness relocation program, where he lives every day in fear that he will be discovered by the organized crime ring that he helped send to . . . Oh, poop.

TURN THE PAGE FOR A SNEAK PEEK AT THE NEXT BOOK ABOUT MILTON AND MARLO'S ADVENTURES IN HECK!

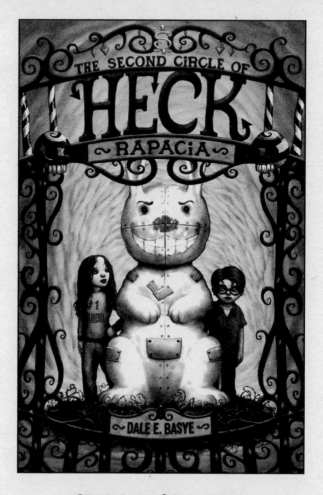

COMING IN JULY 2009!

1 · BLiND AS A BRAT

"OWW . . . YOU FLIPPIN' maniac!" Marlo Fauster shrieked. The demon driver, after untying her hands, had jabbed his pitchspork in a place just south of cordial. Marlo fell to her knees outside the stagecoach and fumbled to remove her blindfold.

The driver, his shape smudged and cloaked in the murky darkness, stood atop the stagecoach and struck a match across his fangs. The bright flare of light felt like an explosion in Marlo's eye sockets.

The driver's nightmarish features burned themselves into the back of Marlo's retinas. Like most of the demons she had met in Heck, he was a creature turned inside out. But this one was even more inside out, somehow: a lanky, walking pizza with everything on it held together by a network of pulsating veins and arteries.

"On second thought"—Marlo gulped—"maybe the blindfold wasn't so bad."

A pale horse with shiny pink eyes clomped nervously in place in front of the stagecoach. The demon driver pompously puffed out his disgusting chest.

"Snatched away in beauty's bloom, on thee shall press no ponderous tomb," he recited in a wet, snooty tone, like a butler with a bronchial infection.

As if things weren't bad enough, Marlo reflected, *now I have to hear his poetry.*

Her eyes adjusted to the light, and she saw she was in some kind of subterranean tunnel. She stood up, brushing gravel off her baggy, sequined #1 GRANDMA sweatshirt and sagging turquoise stirrup pants.

After her brother Milton's unprecedented escape at the Gates of Heck, Marlo had been forced at sporkpoint into this ugly Rapacia uniform, blindfolded, and shoved into the stagecoach of some poetic cadaver.

The next thing Marlo knew, she was here—wherever "here" was. "You are *so* not getting a tip," she said.

The demon folded his arms together smugly. The mesh of winding red and blue capillaries made him appear as if he were a living, throbbing road map. Watching the creature's pulse made Marlo's own pulse quicken.

"My, aren't we a brave little girl?" the demon mocked before suddenly leaping to the ground.

Startled, Marlo jumped back, hitting something with a clang. *"Dang!"* she cursed, rubbing the back of her skull. The demon laughed.

She turned to glare at what had connected with her head so painfully.

UNWELCOME TO RAPACIA, read a sign atop an ornate, metal gate. Twin wrought-iron fleurs-de-lis were welded against a gleaming brass serpent, double curved into a shiny letter "s." At the side of the gate, attached to a crisscross of iron bars, was a large metal box, with a message etched across it: PLEASE LEAVE ALL VALUABLES AND EXPENSIVE PERSONAL EFFECTS HERE SO THAT THEY CAN BE, UM, STORED AND GIVEN BACK TO YOU AT THE END OF ETERNITY.

Marlo peered down the tunnel past the open gate. The passage grew darker in progressively blacker rings that formed a big, black, fathomless eye. She shivered.

"You'd better pick up the pace," the demon jeered. "The Grabbit doesn't like to be kept waiting."

Marlo turned back toward the exploded, overmicrowaved Hot-Pocket-of-a-man.

"The Grabbit?" she asked. "What's a *Grabbit?*"

The demon laughed. "The Grabbit is your new assistant principal. It's what makes Rapacia such an . . . interesting place of torment for greedy, grasping little moppets such as yourself."

The demon turned toward his stagecoach. The creepy white horse "nayed" with a deranged titter.

A wave of panic washed over Marlo.

"What am I supposed to do, you . . . you . . . *freaky carcass* thing?" Marlo shouted into the dark, her chest tight with fear.

The demon sneered over his sinewy shoulder.

"The name is Byron . . . *Lord* Byron," he replied haughtily, his inside-outside body flushed with indignation. "I once wore my heart on my sleeve and now must wear it draped outside my chest, a palpitating medallion for all to see."

The demon chuckled.

"But at least I'm not a naughty little girl—alone—*in the dark.*"

Marlo could practically hear Lord Byron's uncaring shrug as the demon stalked back to the stagecoach, muttering another depressing poem.

After a few long seconds of complete silence, Marlo's ears were suddenly assaulted with the sounds of hooves clacking, wheels squeaking, and monstrous snorts. Slowly, the noises flattened into fading echoes, leaving behind nothing but Marlo's frantic panting.